PROLOGUE

Twelve years ago

FARRELL WOLFE STUMBLED out of the journalism building and squinted at the bright sunlight. Man, he needed a cup of coffee, or two, and a handful of paracetamol. What he didn't need was the upcoming mid-morning lecture from Professor Chen about ethics in journalism—or the human limpet currently superglued to his arm.

He squinted at the feminine hand gripping his biceps. The tall brunette had latched onto him as he'd unfurled his long body out of his seat at the back of the lecture hall, and he dimly recalled her blurry face. He hadn't slept with her last night, right? No, he'd left the club with Damon, and he'd crashed at his place. He'd been, uncharacteristically, alone. Had he picked her up after his five-a-side rugby game a few nights ago? Or at the club he went to earlier in the week? Maybe?

'Last night you mentioned that you were

spending a couple of weeks on your father's yacht in the Seychelles,' she gushed, make-up perfect and hair ruthlessly straightened. Tall, skinny, dressed in blood-vessel-constricting jeans and a very skimpy top. Farrell looked down to see that he was still in his club clothes. He noticed a faint stain on his shirt and remembered someone jostling his hand and spilling his tequila shot. He inhaled, and there it was, the smell of agave and alcohol. His stomach rolled up his throat, and he swallowed his dry heave.

'I would love to join you.'

Farrell lifted his head and looked at her through bleary eyes. What was she going on about? 'Your yacht? In the Seychelles? Will you invite me?' she clarified. 'Summer break is coming up…'

He'd rather shove a hot poker up his nose. The brunette—God, what was her name?—was just another in a line of pretty girls orbiting him and his equally polished circle of friends. Too thin, too high maintenance, too glossy…too eager to please. Too obvious.

A wave of cynicism crashed over him. Yep, he was the full package: tall enough to see over everyone's head, a decent body, a good-looking face and enough family money to make a small country jealous. He was the heir to Wolfe International, a chain of luxury resorts scattered

Passport to Paradise

Final destination: happily-ever-after!

The heat is rising, adventure is calling...
So why not strap in and get swept away to the
world's most luxurious locations? Lands of white sands,
blue skies—and sizzling nights...

Follow our intrepid travelers as they check their
baggage and lose themselves in first-class romance. But
are their connections just for the summer...or are these
jet-setters en route to their five-star forever afters?

Grab your ticket for...

Marriage Ruse in Paradise by Susan Meier

Hired for One Tuscan Summer by Jessica Gilmore

Faking It for the Cameras by Justine Lewis

Surprise Reunion in Croatia by Ella Hayes

One Bed Between Rivals by Joss Wood

Available now!

Her Big Fake Greek Wedding Date by Michele Renae

Coming next month!

Dear Reader,

I love Africa with the heat of a thousand suns, so I'm thrilled to take you to the Seychelles, for a beach holiday between the pages.

Thea has made a career out of keeping her distance. As an award-winning travel blogger, she drifts through the world's most exclusive destinations—observing, never belonging. Detachment keeps her safe, and no one ever tested that more than Farrell Wolfe, her infuriatingly privileged university nemesis. Then she steps off the seaplane at a Seychelles island resort and walks straight into Farrell—now a billionaire hotelier and face of Wolfe International. Thanks to a booking mix-up and a tropical storm, she's stuck sharing a villa with him. He still makes her pulse spike...just not for the same reasons.

But Farrell isn't the arrogant golden boy she remembers. Beneath the gloss, he's fighting to rebuild—and cleaning up his father's corrupt legacy. As storms rage inside and out, Thea and Farrell slip from old rivalry into something dangerously real. And in doing so, they both learn that the greatest adventure isn't running from connection— it's risking everything for something real.

I hope you enjoy my island-based romance. I absolutely loved writing it.

Happy reading!

With my very warm wishes,

Joss
xxx

Instagram: @josswoodbooks
Facebook: @JossWoodAuthor
TikTok: @JossWoodbooks

ONE BED
BETWEEN RIVALS

JOSS WOOD

ROMANCE

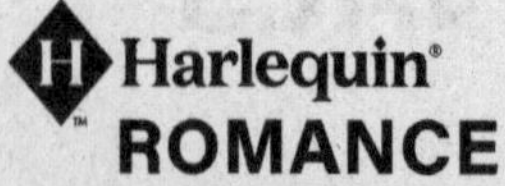

Harlequin® ROMANCE

ISBN-13: 978-1-335-47092-8

One Bed Between Rivals

Recycling programs for this product may not exist in your area.

Harlequin Enterprises ULC
22 Adelaide St. West, 41st Floor
Toronto, Ontario M5H 4E3, Canada
www.Harlequin.com

HarperCollins Publishers
Macken House, 39/40 Mayor Street Upper,
Dublin 1, D01 C9W8, Ireland
www.HarperCollins.com

Printed in U.S.A.

1 2 3 4 5 6 7 8 9 10 HDC 28 27 26 25

Joss Wood loves books, coffee, wine and traveling—especially to the wild places of Southern Africa and, well, anywhere. Joss is a mom to two young adults, and occasionally attempts to grow things, with very mixed (mostly bad) results. She and her husband are bossed around by two cats and a Great Dane that is the size of a small cow. After a career in sales, local economic development and business advocacy, Joss writes full-time from her home in KwaZulu-Natal, South Africa.

Books by Joss Wood

Harlequin Romance

For Business...or Pleasure

Harlequin Presents

Scandals of the Le Roux Wedding

The Billionaire's One-Night Baby
The Powerful Boss She Craves
The Twin Secret She Must Reveal

Cape Town Tycoons

The Nights She Spent with the CEO
The Baby Behind Their Marriage Merger

Hot Winter Escapes

A Nine-Month Deal with Her Husband

A Diamond in the Rough

The Tycoon's Diamond Demand

Hired for the Billionaire's Secret Son
Fast-Track Dating Deception

Visit the Author Profile page
at Harlequin.com for more titles.

across the world, destinations where the rich, famous and infamous went to party and play. His success, it was said, was written in the stars. Or decided by his last name. Even if he got the worst grades on the course—and he never did because he had a photographic memory and information simply stuck—he'd be labelled a success.

Being hungover always made him more introspective. And morose. All he wanted was to find the nearest horizontal surface and pass out.

Farrell shoved his hand into the inner pocket of his leather jacket, hoping to find a pair of sunglasses. Squinting, he watched the door to the journalism building open. Thea Monroe walked down the steps, her arms, as always, filled with books, papers and God knew what else. Strands of her deep brown hair, shot with natural red highlights, had escaped from her messy bun and tumbled over her too-thin shoulders in haphazard curls. The blue smudges under her big grey eyes, light and far too perceptive, were darker than normal and looked like twin bruises on her pale skin. She looked, as she always did, completely exhausted and resolutely fierce.

Farrell pinched the bridge of his nose, hating the way she always managed to make him feel…useless, indulgent, careless. Which, let's be honest, he was.

She was everything he tried not to think about—dedicated, hardworking, annoyingly idealistic. Morally upright to the point of ridiculousness. Thea's sense of right and wrong was practically carved in stone, while he'd been taught that morals were fluid: shapeable, negotiable, bendable for the sake of the family's comfort. The Wolfes didn't break rules—they just moved the lines that didn't suit them.

Thea was his only real rival on the course, sharp-eyed, faster than him in thought. She challenged him and made him think. Worse—she made him care. Care about being better, about paying attention, about being…interested. Which was, frankly, very, very annoying.

'Monroe, it's nearly the end of term. Take a breath, why don't you? You don't have to try so damn hard,' he muttered.

Those grey eyes met his, and drilled straight through him, powering through his ribcage, landing in his heart, and scorching his soul. Her eyes raked over him, and he couldn't help lifting his hand to his stubbled face, wishing his eyes didn't look so bloodshot, and that he didn't look as if he'd got to bed at around four in the morning, completely shattered by too many tequilas.

Her eyes were too big for her thin face—heart-shaped and elfin—and her full, sexy, and unpainted lips were pursed. She wore old jeans, older basketball trainers and a slouchy sweater revealing one collarbone. A part of him wanted to kiss her, another part of him wanted to wrap his arms around her, while another wanted to march her off to the nearest takeaway and feed her a couple of hamburgers, a double-chocolate shake and a basket of chips. She annoyed him, but he also felt strangely protective of her. Weird, because usually nobody in the Wolfe family cared about anyone but themselves.

He didn't like it. He didn't like himself whenever she was around. Or, to be fair, he liked himself less when she was around.

'Just do us all a favour and take a break,' he muttered. 'Who are you trying to impress?' He delivered the words in a lazy drawl, but he ached inside…a combination of too much alcohol and too little sleep. And, possibly, a stream of underlying discontentment, and a layer of shame.

The papers in Thea's hands slipped, and a sheet of paper drifted to the ground. He recognised Professor Chen's handwriting and raised his eyebrows at his extensive notes. He'd never been given the same input from their professor; then again, his work didn't need much critiquing. Yes, he had the advantage of having a photographic memory, but Thea put in the work… Farrell rocked on his feet, uncomfortable. Was it his fault he'd been gifted with an eidetic memory? Why should he feel bad about it?

'Bravo, Farrell, really. It's a talent to casually dole out insults with a hangover while your father bulldozes reefs and buys his way out of lawsuits.'

He'd heard the rumours, he wasn't that out of touch, and he occasionally checked in with his dad and what Wolfe International was up to. He'd been told the two or three minor reports about environmental abuses that had made it to print were wildly over-exaggerated. Getting bashed by the environmentalists was par for the course.

'Where are you getting your information, Red—from Hugging-Trees-R-Us?' he mocked. 'You are doing a journalism degree; you should know better than to believe everything you read.'

Her chin lifted. 'If you actually paid attention for once, you might start realising the damage your family has done.'

He gritted his teeth. 'Wolfe Industries is clean,' he insisted.

'And your head is buried in the sand—how's the view down there?' she asked, her eyes raking him from head to toe. 'It must be lovely to live in a sanitised, wealthy world, Wolfe.'

Her mocking tone felt like nails on a chalkboard. He groaned and touched his aching head.

'God, can you step off your pedestal for a minute, please?'

'But I like the view from up here,' she retorted. 'And at least I live in the real world, without my daddy funding my way and making life easier for me.'

Her words landed, sharp and pointed, each one tipped with acid and burning into his skin. Man, she knew exactly where to hurl those verbal knives. He couldn't deny his dad's money paid for his luxury flat, his sports car, the designer threads, the partying. He was twenty-four years old, but he suddenly felt sixteen, small, inconsequential, diminished. He didn't like it.

But he couldn't let any of that show, not when he had an audience. He looked down and took in the brunette's quizzical expression; it was obvious she'd lost track of the conversation. He released a low chuckle, dredged from his vast repertoire of acting skills—showing any emotion in front of his father was like tossing chum into shark-infested waters—and forced his shoulders to drop.

Thea saw too much, knew too much. She was far too intuitive and way too stubborn. Her tiny frame was mostly made up of unshakable, infuriating integrity. Thea Monroe didn't bend or buckle. Not for him, nor, he presumed, anyone else.

'You are why Hollywood makes movies about rich guys getting their comeuppance, Wolfe,' she told him, before shifting the bundle in her arms and handing him another scathing look. Then she walked away, leaving him standing in the too-bright sun, feeling as if she'd taken a bite out of him, chewed him up, and spat him back out.

'What the hell is her problem?' his companion asked, pouting.

'Who knows?' he replied, still pretending he didn't give a damn, and that Thea didn't leave him feeling scratchy and annoyed.

But as Thea walked away, he slapped a hand to his chest, trying—and failing—to rub away the burning sensation under his ribcage. Not being a fan of introspection, he pushed himself to identify the emotions drilling through his soul. Resentment, sure, for letting her get to him, and for provoking a reaction. Envy, absolutely, because she believed in something bigger than herself, something better. And…crap…he hated to admit it, but attraction too. Damn her. Because she was seriously impressive.

'So, is that a yes for the Seychelles?'

CHAPTER ONE

THEA PRESSED HER forehead to the oval plane window, unable to stop her breath hitching. Nor could she stop the acceleration of her heartbeat. She'd seen pictures of the Seychelles a thousand times before—in brochures, online and in glossy magazines, in Instagram feeds dripping with a 'look at me, I'm perfect' attitude. Yet nothing had prepared her for the view below the sixteen-seater small plane ferrying her and her fellow journalists to Petit Saphir. The small islands north of Anse Reunion, somewhere between the east coast of Grand Anse and Felicite, were scattered jewels on an endless ocean, hugged by pale, powdered beaches, almost aggressively perfect. The sea wasn't one shade of blue, but a dozen—cobalt at the horizon, glassclear at the shore, turquoise in between. It was as if Mother Nature hadn't been able to settle on a colour and had decided to use all the shades of blue in her paintbox.

With another swoop of the plane, Petit Saphir

revealed itself, again almost too pretty, almost too perfect. It looked like an AI image, born out of the prompts of a travel marketer who'd had too many espressos, someone who'd typed the words 'tropical paradise' too many times. From Thea's seat above the island, Petit Saphir wore a lush green crown, edged with granite boulders and soft curving beaches of white sand. Hidden coves glittered in the sun, and tucked into the southern end was the resort itself: low golden buildings stitched into the hillside, roofs blending with palm trees. It felt as if the architect had taken luxury, the beach and the jungle and knitted them together.

It was breathtaking. And it made her suspicious. Because beauty this polished always came at a cost. And maybe also because it was owned by Wolfe International, the holding company owned and operated by Farrell Wolfe, her university nemesis.

He'd been older than most of their class, thanks to a three-year gap studying in the States. Farrell didn't just waltz through life—he glided, with a ridiculous sophistication that made the rest of them look as if they were still figuring out which fork to use. She'd hated him immediately and utterly loathed the squirrelly feeling in her stomach whenever he'd wandered into her vicinity.

She'd rolled her eyes at his designer watch, his K-drama-inspired, effortlessly stylish clothes, the cool smirk daring the world not to fall at his feet. She'd had no time for the pretty or the shallow, and she still didn't. But now and again, and far too rarely, his fir-green eyes turned a little haunted, and the tightness of his sexy mouth suggested some genuine feelings. She recalled, with perfect clarity, how he'd raked his fingers through his long, sun-streaked hair as if he was trying to erase a thought—or a memory. It made her wonder if his golden life was really as incredible as it looked.

And his brain… *Man*, his brain. He'd already finished a degree in business and had been adding some marketing, PR and journalism classes to round off his education. When he'd cared about something—when that gnat-like attention had landed on something he'd found fascinating—he'd dazzled. His eyes had sparkled, his rugged features had softened, and his words had quickened and flowed, transforming him into someone fascinating, someone compelling, a man she'd ached to know.

And it drove her mad that she'd wanted to. Thankfully, that feeling had soon passed because he'd catch himself, his expression would shutter, and he'd make a sarcastic or flippant remark, heralding the return of the jerk she'd hated…

Had he changed? Or was he still the self-involved cretin she remembered all too well? Thea shrugged, knowing she wasn't destined to have her question answered. As CEO and majority shareholder of a global resort empire, he'd almost certainly hand this promo tour—a ten-day stay on Petit Saphir to show off his latest project—to his PR team. Entertaining journalists was *way* beneath his pay grade.

Thea checked her seat belt and, rolling her shoulders, reminded herself that it didn't matter who owned the resort; she was concerned only about the visitor experience. That was all she ever reported on. She was regarded as one of the few unbiased travel bloggers around, with a reputation for fairness, and she had a loyal following as a result. And these days, when accommodation establishments wanted to promote their newest offerings, she made the list.

Every day, she received many emails requesting her to review places, but when the email had dropped into her inbox from Wolfe International's PR team, inviting her to review Petit Saphir—for five or ten days, her choice—she'd jumped at the chance and accepted the longer stay. Partly because it was reputed to be WI's most impressive development yet, partly because she wanted to see whether the company lived up to their promise of being ecologically sustainable—she'd heard rumours of greenwashing; like many others, WI was rumoured to market their resorts as being environmentally responsible without making meaningful changes to reduce environmental harm. She wanted to find out whether they were living up to all their promises.

And sure, she was curious about Farrell Wolfe—who wouldn't be?

Farrell aside, she was visiting one of the premier island destinations in the world. She had, bar none, the best job in the world, one she'd never believed was possible all those years ago, living in that horrible house in Bristol with her equally awful parents. What would they think about her job? Would they be impressed? No, probably not. Very little about her had ever impressed them, and there had been so little about her they'd liked. And that was why she'd dropped out of their lives.

Love had always been a conditional thing—sunshine one day, storm clouds the next. She'd learned early that leaning on someone came with a price: disappointment, withdrawal, the sudden absence of the people who were supposed to be steadfast. She couldn't remember a time when she'd felt emotionally safe with her parents, and she'd walked an emotional high wire all her life. With no safety net.

She'd learned that it was safer to step back, to observe, to watch rather than engage. Intimacy felt like exposure and vulnerability a steel-toothed trap.

She now understood that her parents were narcissists, drawn together in mutual admiration over how much damage they could inflict. She'd been in her teens, fourteen or fifteen, when she'd realised—after a particularly confusing and hurtful fight—that her parents were like two evil, feral cats and she was the mouse they loved to toy with. Realising she needed to leave had saved her in more ways than she could count. After consulting a school psychologist, she'd planned her exit strategy, how she could survive, what steps to take. Then, at sixteen, she'd applied to the courts to become an emancipated teen, and at sixteen and a half, she'd mentally, physically and financially divorced herself from her parents. Oh, it had been a long, hard struggle, but she knew that if she'd stayed, she might now be… God, broken? Yeah, broken wasn't an exaggeration. Shattered was an even better word.

'Folks,' the captain's smooth voice broke into her thoughts, 'we have to wait for the other seaplane to land and disembark, so we have a little time on our hands. How about an aerial tour of Grande Saphir?'

Always keen to look at something new, Thea

looked out of her small window and watched as they approached another, bigger island. From her research, she knew that Grande Saphir was the big-brother island to Petit Saphir. As they flew low over the charming, tiny harbour, she noticed that this island was less touristy, with fishermen's nets on the harbour wall, small shops and stalls selling fruit. They flew up the beach, and Thea watched a couple walking on the soft sand, hand in hand, engrossed in each other. Seeing them, she was both envious and terrified. Envious of their ability to take such a chance on loving someone, terrified of putting herself in the firing line to be loved and insulted, loved and denigrated, loved and left. A part of her wanted the connection, wanted the fairy tale, but the risk felt too high. To need someone was to risk being left behind, and she had enough experience to know how much that hurt. So, she stayed on the safe side of things. Observing. Recording. Writing other people's stories while keeping her feelings and her past locked away.

Thea smiled at a little boy sprinting naked across the sand, his father chasing him with a pair of tiny board shorts. She noticed the glossy braids of a striking local woman, the unapologetic curves of her body displayed in a neon-pink bikini. The water the woman waded through was so clear that Thea felt she could count every grain of sand beneath her feet.

She kept looking out of the window as the plane banked, unable to tear her eyes away from the palm trees and brightly painted houses below. Travel writing had always been her shield—her way of being in the world without fully stepping into it. And for years, too many now, she'd told herself that it was enough.

But lately it didn't feel like it. She felt suspended, waiting, as if she'd been travelling the world looking for…something. Not love—that was far too dramatic—but a spark, a shift, a reason to feel different. She hadn't found it at the slick ski resort in Utah, or exploring the streets of Cartagena, or even beneath the neon lights of Tokyo. So why did some part of her hope she'd find that elusive something while visiting this remote island off the coast of Africa?

Farrell Wolfe looked out to sea and tipped his head, taking in the extensive blue skies and the blazing sun. The sea looked lake-calm, and nothing suggested a massive storm was moving in from the north-east and would pummel the island in a matter of hours.

He looked at his second in command, and best friend. He and Kyle had started at Wolfe Industries at the same time, and somehow, despite being the owner's son and an employee, became friends. Kyle, on realising that he was competing against—in his words—a nepo baby, had made the strategic decision to work with Farrell instead of against him, and over the past decade they'd made a formidable team. Kyle was a details guy, someone who could take his grand ideas and boil them down to their nuts and bolts, financial or otherwise. If Kyle said a project wasn't viable, Farrell always, always listened. He was the only person he trusted.

'Do you have an update on the storm?'

Kyle lifted his head, taking his eyes off his phone's screen. They'd been tracking a tropical storm for days now, and everyone was on edge, unable to believe that they'd have to deal with a massive storm on the day their first guests were due to arrive. They'd had many discussions as to whether they should postpone or not. But it had taken six months to settle on this date, and he and Kyle had eventually decided to go ahead regardless of the weather. As long as the seaplanes could deliver their guests and return to Mahé safely, they'd be able to ride out the storm. He'd built the resort to withstand most of what the weather and ocean could throw at them—the cabins and the majority of the resort were on stilts, safe from high waves or, God forbid, in extreme circumstances, a tsunami.

The buildings were reinforced for hurricanes and high winds…they'd done everything they could. Provided the guests stayed inside for the night, everyone would be fine.

'It's moving in faster than expected,' Kyle told him, a frown between his eyebrows. 'But the planes will be here shortly, and the pilots will definitely be able to return to Mahé safely. They will be flying away from the storm.'

Farrell nodded. 'Has the hurricane strengthened?'

Kyle dragged his finger across the screen, took in some information and nodded. 'Yes. It's going to be brutal, I'm afraid.'

Farrell scanned the horizon for the planes and sighed. 'We've thought of everything, right?' he asked Kyle.

Kyle nodded and smiled. 'Yes. Relax, Farrell.'

He wished he could. 'Did you vet the journalists? No one on the list is going to do a hatchet job, are they?'

Kyle shoved his phone into his shirt pocket. 'All are well respected and have a reputation for balanced reporting. Do you want me to quickly go through their credentials?'

Had he even looked at the list of inbound journalists? If he had, he couldn't remember doing so. These past few months had been mad—he'd been running Wolfe International and his foundation, and overseeing the building of this resort in his favourite place in the world. He'd handed the task of publicising Petit Saphir to Kyle and his publicity director. Besides, the journalists were a few minutes out. If he didn't approve, there was nothing he could do about it now. Farrell shook his head. 'No, it's fine.'

Kyle sent him a tired smile. 'You should see the planes soon. I'm going to head on inside and leave you to do the meet and greet.'

Kyle was a behind-the-scenes person and always faded away when the spotlight switched on. Conversely, Farrell had been standing in the spotlight so long, he barely knew it was there any more. That was the price of being a Wolfe from Wolfe Industries.

To keep himself from smoothing down his shirt, from wiping his slightly damp hands on his thighs, Farrell slid his hands into the pockets of his chino shorts and dug his fingertips into his thighs. He glanced down at his open-neck white linen shirt, untucked and wondered if he should've worn trainers instead of leather flip-flops. Did he look too casual? As if he wasn't taking this preview of the resort seriously?

Grateful for his designer sunglasses, he closed his eyes and tried, as surreptitiously as he could, to take a deep breath. *Calm the hell down, Wolfe, you're acting like a teenager about to go on his first date.* Arriving with the journalists was a small group of new investors. He got only one chance to make a first impression. He wasn't worried about what they would think about the resort—it was perfect, he'd made sure of that—but how they'd react to him and his plans for the next project.

He wondered how much research they'd have done on Wolfe Industries. How far back did they go? Five years, ten? He swallowed. Fifteen? What did they know of the past, and how much?

How much research had they done on him? At university, he'd been every inch the Wolfe heir—handsome, arrogant, untouchable. He'd coasted on charm and a name that opened doors, a golden boy who never questioned the champagne in his glass or the glossy car he drove. He hadn't cared where it all came from. Frankly, he hadn't wanted to know.

That wilful blindness had shattered a couple of years after he'd strolled into Wolfe International in his designer suit, full of swagger. The ultimate, unqualified nepo baby. He'd shadowed his father, and in the process of learning the business, surprisingly, he was better at it than anyone, himself included, had expected. Like everyone else at Wolfe International, he'd ignored the lone protestor who'd appeared outside the building for two weeks straight, waving a placard accusing his father of being a thief, a conman, a man who'd stolen a community's heritage. Then, two years after that, a young woman had taken his place, holding the same placard—pretty, curvy, and very much his type. And very wet from the driving rain.

Bored, and because the day had been quiet, he'd crossed the street and invited her for coffee in the café over the road. An hour later, after hearing her story—and why she'd been standing there instead of her brother—he'd seen the world very differently.

After taking her number and leaving her at the café, he'd gone back to the office, locked the door, and started digging. Twelve hours later, he'd peeled back two decades of rot. Resort after resort built on stolen land. Communities pushed aside or cheated out of their land and homes by slick lawyers and loopholes, all directed by his father. Reefs levelled for better views, and entire ecosystems, mangrove forests, wetlands and forests wiped out. What he'd thought was his inheritance wasn't a legacy—it was devastation disguised under the banner of progress and job creation. And one family in Fiji had paid the highest price.

In confronting who his father was, what he did, Farrell had been forced to look at who he was and what he stood for. And had found out that he liked himself as much as he liked the company…which wasn't much at all. Determined to understand—because how could you go somewhere if you didn't know where you'd been?—he'd tackled his father, demanding answers. Numerous fights had ended with his father suffering a minor stroke. The stroke had triggered early onset dementia, and within a year Farrell had had full control of the WI empire—he'd inherited his father's shares, position and sins. Even if he was the only one who knew—he'd buried all the proof—the stain on his father's name had become his, too.

But Farrell refused to let Wolfe International continue to be associated with wreaking havoc. Fully in charge, he'd poured himself into rewriting its story. Quietly. Deliberately. He'd established a foundation and funnelled money back into the communities previously affected by WI's actions. He'd funded environmental research programmes and ecological restorations. It was difficult to return land, but he'd tried. He didn't talk about or publicise his actions—partly because his dad was still his dad and wasn't in a position to defend his actions, partly because he knew the world would sneer. They'd call it whitewashing, a rich man's guilt dressed up as progress.

He genuinely believed that if he exposed what

he called his 'shadow work', the scandal of his father's many borderline criminal, definitely morally reprehensible actions would not only come to light but undermine, possibly decimate, the progress Farrell had made before it had the chance to matter. Nothing, and no one, would stop, or distract him from turning the Wolfe name into something it had never been before: clean.

Farrell pushed an agitated hand through his hair, rolled his shoulders, then tipped his head from side to side. Why the hell was he so nervous? He wasn't a guy who generally felt on edge…so why now?

He heard the buzz of the seaplanes and lifted his eyes to the sky, quickly picking up two of them making their approach to land. He pulled a smile onto his face and deliberately relaxed his entire body, hoping he was projecting an aura of relaxed calm. *Don't slip. Don't falter. Don't give them a crack to look through and see the mess beneath…*

Appearances, after all, were everything. Hadn't that been drummed into him since the moment he could understand words and gestures? Approval from his father came only through public success, charm, polish, and looking and acting like a Wolfe. Whatever the hell that meant. His looks passed muster, and hours spent at the gym ensured he looked fit. Expertly cut hair, designer stubble, expensive clothes.

He looked what he was…arguably the most astute, successful Wolfe International CEO in three generations. He dated ballet dancers and actresses, models and A-listers, and lived a life most would call perfect. Then why did he feel so hollow? Was it because every privilege he'd coasted on—the cars, the clubs, the careless cruelty—had been bought with stolen land and ruined ecosystems, and, no matter how hard he tried to make it right, no amount of money or green projects could scrub the blemish from his name?

The first seaplane landed and cruised to a stop at the end of the pier, causing deep ripples in the clear water. Its arrival disturbed a ray buried in the sand, and Farrell watched it hustle away. He wished he could do the same. God, he was so tired…

The door to the plane opened and Farrell squared his shoulders, straightened his spine. It was time to turn on the charm, switch to 'perfect host' mode. He could never let anyone, ever, see his vulnerability, the uncertainty beneath his polished exterior. He needed to control the narrative. That was all that was important. Showing someone the mess two layers deep would never happen.

Farrell stepped forward, smiling. He shook the hand of one investor, buzzed the cheek of another. He recognised an extremely famous travel journalist and shook hand after hand. The second plane landed, and the first taxied away to allow the pilot to discharge the second batch of guests. Smiling, Farrell watched, fascinated, as a lean, shapely, feminine leg emerged from under the frothy hem of a floral sundress and her foot hit the pier. He experienced a jolt of recognition as his eyes hit that still familiar face, as he took in her deep auburn hair, cut now to flirt with her shoulders. The sharp assessing eyes, deeply grey and witchy, were still too big for her face, but no less impactful. *She's even more beautiful now.* The jolt of recognition pulsed through him as his body reacted before his brain could restart. Stunning, lovely, now a woman, not a girl…

Thea Monroe.

She lifted her head, looked at him, and, despite the barrier of his sunglasses, electricity sparked between them. Was it left over from the animosity they'd shared at college, or was this new, powered by an instant, unwanted attraction? He didn't know, but he couldn't let her see he was surprised or, worse, that he was attracted. He didn't do unguarded.

Find your smooth smile, display some of that

easy charm you're renowned for. Get it the hell together, Wolfe.

He caught the expensive leather-bound notebook Thea held in her left hand, and saw her at twenty-two, hair a mess, an ink stain on her white top, her hand clutching another, battered spiral notebook, its edge curled and tatty. A notebook, those long legs and slim body, that gorgeous face, the slightest sneer teasing her lips, the chill in her pewter eyes. Some things didn't change.

She'd been able to see through his charm back then; would she be able to still? The thought suddenly terrified him.

He moved in close, planting his frame between her and the rest of the party loitering on the pier, welcome cocktails in their hands, their excited murmurs now indistinguishable, background noise. His finger brushed the corner of her notebook, and he summoned a smile he hoped looked easy, careless.

'Still scribbling by hand? You do know there's tech for that now? Or is this—' his voice tripped, a fraction too sharp '—just your way of pretending you're smarter than me?'

The words dropped, and he instantly wished them back. God, what a pathetic, asinine, childish jab. Twelve years of silence, and that was what he led with? He felt the heat of shame crawl under his collar. Why did she still do this to him? How was she able to strip away the polish, slice straight to the man he worked so hard to bury?

Thea didn't so much as blink. With a clean flick of her wrist, she slid the notebook out of his reach and dropped it to rest against her thigh, her eyes flat, cool, unamused.

'No,' she said, her voice a blade. 'Just wiser than the boy who once believed—and probably still does—that charm could pass for substance.'

CHAPTER TWO

Thea released her pent-up breath as Farrell turned away to greet another guest. Typical Farrell—the words rolled off his tongue, sharp and smug, still determined to sneak under her skin. And, damn him, she'd almost let them.

But she'd managed, thanks to her parents' training, not to react. Her pulse might've skipped, but her face stayed cool, her voice steady.

For once, her retort had been on point. And judging by the way his confident mask had flickered for a split second, she knew she'd knocked him back, just a fraction. With that knowledge came a grim, quiet satisfaction. He could still push her buttons, but, clearly, she could push his harder.

He was here, on the island, not in some office somewhere. Older, obviously, bigger, harder… possibly meaner, too. Thea's fingers curled tight around her notebook—it was something solid, something grounding. *God.* Farrell Wolfe.

Twelve years of silence and then he was suddenly there, striding towards her with that same infuriating swagger. And, of course, the first words out of his mouth had to be a jab. Arrogant. Juvenile. So very…him.

But she'd seen it—the flicker in his eyes when she'd retaliated, the stumble beneath the smooth exterior. For a second, the golden boy, now the golden man, had looked human. And that unsettled her. *He* unsettled her.

She pressed her lips together, annoyed. She wasn't who she was before—the girl who'd veered between confusion and curiosity, annoyance and attraction. She'd hated his casual attitude but had loved his sharp-as-a-scalpel mind, and his way of looking at the world, an issue, a problem, in an interesting way. She'd caught him looking at her once or twice, his expression puzzled, as if he didn't know what to make of her, curiosity in his eyes.

Then, just when she thought he was redeemable, that she'd judged him too harshly, he'd toss a careless, cutting comment her way, casually cruel. She'd walk away, her pride bruised, and she'd lie awake that night, and for many nights following, wishing she had a better, perfect comeback. A sharper insult. So why was her heart doing a flat-out sprint? And why did his voice, smug and low, make her feel as if he were pressing an old bruise?

Thea straightened her spine. He was a part of her past; she'd moved on. And whatever guilt, shame or regret Farrell Wolfe was experiencing—if any at all—was his problem, not hers.

Thea hung at the back of the crowd, her backpack over her shoulder, the sun beating down on her head as she watched Farrell meet and greet his guests with practised charm. The sun picked up blond highlights in his brown hair, and while she couldn't see his green eyes behind those ridiculously expensive shades, she suspected she'd see tiny lines feathering the corners. His chest definitely seemed wider, his biceps under that short-sleeved shirt thicker and more, yeah, biteable.

Thea turned away to look at the big rocks standing like sentries in the transparent sea, the long wooden pier perfectly placed between two of the biggest boulders. She placed her hand on her stomach, unaccustomed to it hopping around like a bunny on speed. What was wrong with her? Why was she reacting this way? Yes, Wolfe was a good-looking guy—no, he was a great-looking guy!—but he was also a product of inherited wealth, privilege and arrogance.

There were twenty-plus people on the pier, and everyone had picked up a brightly coloured cocktail from the trays of waiters dressed in khaki shorts and matching black golf shirts. It was barely twelve, hot, hot, hot, and she was a redhead. Running into Farrell again was problematic enough; she didn't need to add alcohol to the mix. She needed water. And her hat. But she'd forgotten to pack her sunglasses.

She sipped her cocktail and pulled a face. It was slightly too sweet, and why were they still standing here, getting roasted by the sun? Their bags had disappeared, so they should be being ushered up to what she hoped would be a cool reception area, preferably with the aircon blasting. *You're not here to look for faults, Monroe, you can't be biased from the get-go. You have to keep your distance, your emotions corralled, any revived irritation at bay.* She was here to do a job, to report on this island resort with no bias. It was why she had a huge social media following, why she was trusted to tell the truth. She never allowed her personal feelings to get in the way of the truth.

If this resort lived up to its promises—six-star accommodation and amenities, Michelin-worthy food, being properly eco-friendly, community participation, sensitivity to the environment— she'd gladly, okay, maybe not gladly, report the truth and nothing but the truth.

She glared at Farrell's broad back. It might

test her, but being tested was good for personal growth, right?

Thea's eyes dipped before she could stop them, landing on his butt—still gorgeous, damn it. She tried to will away her appreciation, tried to ignore the little hitch in her breath, the ridiculous flutter in her chest, the way her heart ricocheted off her ribs. Her body still liked his… It hadn't learned a single thing in twelve years. The sun turned his stubble golden, and she wondered whether he was tanned from hours spent in this water, or from running on the beach.

She released a tiny snort. He was a businessman, a high-flying CEO, he probably only ever worked out in state-of-the-art gyms and spent time on a sunbed. Or was she just assuming that because it made her feel better to think badly of him? Thea rubbed the back of her neck and grimaced at the beads of sweat on her fingertips. She really needed to get out of the sun. Preferably immediately.

'Drink this, Thea,' Farrell quietly stated, plucking her glass from her hand and pushing another into it. His fingers brushed hers, and she lifted her eyes to look up. And up. She'd forgotten how tall he was…nearly a foot taller than her five three. It was hard to pull her eyes off his face to look down at the glass he'd handed her.

'No, thanks,' she muttered, trying to shove it back.

His fingers held hers to the glass. 'It's non-alcoholic and, believe it or not, at its base, it's a rehydrating drink. Citrus, salt, and some honey. Most guests can't handle the summer heat, so we hand these out like…' his sexy mouth quirked up into that half-smile she remembered so well '…water. Drink it.'

She couldn't think of a reason not to, and he was right: she was thirsty. She lifted the drink and gulped, loving the fresh citrus, the ice and the way it soothed her parched throat. She gripped the glass with both hands and watched as Farrell took off his shades, pulling back slightly when he moved to place them over her eyes.

'You're squinting. It's going to give you a headache,' he told her, lightly pressing his finger on its bridge to keep the shades on her face. 'You probably have one already, because your eyes are so light and the sun bounces off the ocean.'

Well, yes, but how did he know that? He never used to be this observant. 'You need to wear a hat whenever you are outside,' he stated, once again pushing the too-big sunglasses up her nose.

'I have one in my bag,' she muttered, after draining the last few sips of her drink. As soon as she lowered the glass, Farrell gestured for a waiter to step forward, and he picked up another glass. 'Get that in you.'

Before she could reply, he removed the backpack from her shoulder and opened the zip. Thea wanted to protest, but he was too fast for her. His hand slid inside and rooted around. 'What are you doing?' she whispered, conscious of the attention they were attracting from the other guests.

He peered inside and removed a floppy cotton hat. 'Bingo.' He slapped the hat on her head and draped her backpack over his shoulder.

'Farrell…' Thea warned, adjusting the hat with her free hand so that she could see out from behind his expensive lenses. 'Everyone is watching us.'

Farrell lifted his sandy eyebrows, turned slowly and eyed his guests. Thea wondered if they caught his small jolt of surprise; it was almost as if he'd forgotten they were there. That charming smile, the one that didn't reach his eyes, widened, and he dragged his hand through his hair. He placed a big hand on her shoulder, sending a buzz of…what was that? *Electricity?*… down her arm. 'Thea and I were at uni together, we've known each other for ever,' he announced.

Wow, now, that wasn't the truth. Okay, it was, but… They'd attended the same classes and known of each other. Their interactions had been limited to trading insults and glares. She hadn't seen him since their graduation ceremony, where he'd been swallowed up by his friends and family. The last time she'd laid eyes on him, he'd been posing for a photograph, scroll in hand, gown on, mortarboard tipped at a rakish angle, many of their fellow graduates surrounding him, his father watching from the side.

She'd been, as she always was, alone.

A ripple of understanding ran through the crowd, and Farrell, still holding her backpack, gestured for them to follow him. 'Let's get out of this hot sun, folks. Like I told Thea, the sun can be brutal. If you feel light-headed or a little strange, let one of us know; it's easy to get sunstroke.' He glanced at Thea, his eyes raking over her. 'Redheads are particularly susceptible.'

Thea sent him a hot glare but knew it was ineffective as most of her face was covered by his sunglasses and the rim of her hat. She'd glare at him later, properly, when she could make her feelings clear.

It would be great if she knew exactly what her feelings were.

'Welcome to Petit Saphir,' Farrell said, gesturing for them to precede him up the pier. 'We're planning on making it a very fun ten days.'

Fun. With him. How would that be possible

when she was wobbling between exasperation, outrage, and a heartbeat that refused to behave? She didn't trust him…and, worse, for the first time since she'd left home, she didn't fully trust herself around him.

And she absolutely, positively, did not want to admit that a part of her couldn't wait to see what came next.

'You can give me Ms Monroe's room key, and I'll escort her to her villa.'

Farrell held out his hand and frowned at the panicked look in his manager's eyes. Why did she look as if he were about to chew her up and spit her out? Out of the corner of his eye, he saw Thea walking from the restroom, the hem of her dress swishing against her slim thighs. He'd arranged it so that she was served last, and the rest of his guests were on their way to their villas, escorted by his competent and charming staff. He intended to show Thea to her villa himself.

Partly because he didn't want to leave her yet, but mostly because he needed to apologise for his stupid, cutting comment on the pier, to show her he wasn't the arrogant, entitled bastard she remembered. He shut his eyes, shame crashing over his head, searing his cheeks, and prickling the back of his neck. He was the CEO of a global company, a man who managed a dozen crises before breakfast—yet he'd reverted to a sulky kid the moment Thea had looked at him. Shame wasn't a stranger; it was an old companion, courtesy of his father. But he'd always been able to keep a sliver of distance, reminding himself that he was trying to be better, do better. With Thea, though—both then and now—his actions had been indefensible.

He needed to apologise.

Crap. He was a guy who preferred to speak via actions, not words. *Just get it done, Wolfe.*

'Um…sir?'

He focused on his manager's face, taking in her warm brown skin and panicked eyes. 'Problem?' He didn't know why he'd asked; he'd already realised something was wrong.

'Well, we've run out of villas.'

What? How could they…?

'I don't understand,' he said, striving for patience. He darted a glance at Thea. She stood in front of the massive, extensive, floor-to-ceiling window overlooking the boulders standing in the sea, bisected by a tiny beach. Thea looked captivated by the storm that had rolled in while he and his guests had enjoyed a very late lunch. He could sense the electricity, tasted the faintest hint of copper in the air and knew the world, definitely this island, was holding its breath, waiting for the storm to break. Big, fat, shotgun-like raindrops hit the roof and the windows... There it was, the opening salvo. Thunder rolled, and Farrell glanced at his watch. He had, maybe, five minutes to get Thea to her villa before she got drenched. Since golf carts were the only motorised transport on the island, he was resigned to getting wet no matter what he did.

'Well, Mr Gumede, after assuring us that he was travelling solo, arrived with his wife and daughter. We had to do a major reshuffle of rooms, but we are still short a room.'

John Gumede was a major investor in many of Farrell's past projects, including Petit Saphir, and a big part of his future plans. Whatever the man needed, he'd informed his staff, he got. Immediately. Including an extra room for his daughter.

Hell. Why hadn't he noticed two extra people on the pier earlier? Oh, that would be because his brain had been full of Thea, digesting her sudden reappearance in his life, then worried about the sheen of perspiration on her face, the beating of the pulse in her neck. He hadn't noticed anything but her. Farrell silently released a string of curse words.

'What options do we have?' he demanded.

'None, and that's why I've already allocated the guests' rooms and sent them on their way. There was no point in telling them about our faux pas.'

Technically, it was Gumede's faux pas, but Farrell would never tell him that.

'Bottom line is, we are out of rooms. Ms Monroe is a highly influential travel journalist, and making her sleep on the couch would give a very bad impression.'

Farrell gripped the counter, his fingers turning white. He was so screwed. Thunder boomed, and he looked beyond Thea to see the storm had properly started its onslaught now, battering the island with savage rain. It had gone from zero to a hundred in a few minutes: wind howled through the palms, bending them low, rain slicing sideways in sheets so dense he could barely see the beach and the boulders. The storm needled him—the sheer, unapologetic wildness of it. It wasn't polished, was out of control, and it had no rhyme or reason to it. Just raw force, the kind that stripped everything bare. And damn if it didn't feel uncomfortably familiar, the same sensation he'd had the moment Thea's grey eyes had found his again—as if she were another storm created just for him.

He heard his manager's sigh. 'Not only are we a room short, but there is also no way the guests will make it back here for the welcoming dinner,' she said. If the storm had been a typical summer squall, his staff would've simply ushered guests to and from their rooms beneath massive umbrellas. But his staff weren't typical—they were the best in the world, trained to anticipate every hiccup. So, while the rain lashed down, the dining tables in the villas gleamed, perfectly set silver cloches hiding a feast. Imported charcuterie boards, chilled vichyssoise, lobster salad, and a jewel-box selection of miniature desserts waited, decadent and flawless, ready for his guests when they wanted to eat. It was the best anyone could do during a major hurricane.

But, in the meantime, he had to figure out what to do with Thea…

Actually, he had only one option, one he'd been avoiding since hearing the bad news. He had a private villa on the island, tucked into the far corner of the property, as far away from the lodge and guests as he could get. It was a one-bedroom villa, with extraordinary views, as luxurious as any in the resort. She could sleep in his bedroom, and he'd sleep on the couch downstairs. Had he ever slept on anyone's couch, ever? He gripped the bridge of his nose and closed his eyes. He didn't believe so.

As they said, there was a first time for everything.

With Farrell's hand on her back, Thea ran through the stinging rain to a recessed wooden front door, grateful when he reached past her shoulder and pushed it open. The ride over in the golf cart had been longer than she thought, and she was soaked through. Even her bra and panties were wet, and her sandals squelched on the tiles of the double-volume entrance hall. Thea pushed her wet hair off her forehead and shivered, turning slowly to take in the impressive villa. The hall led into a great room, a kitchen ran into a dining area, which morphed into a huge sitting area, populated with comfortable, large couches, a massive flat screen on the wall and floor-to-ceiling windows, which led—she squinted—onto what she thought was a wooden deck. Between the inky light and the storm, it was hard to tell what was beyond the huge glass panes. After squeezing water out of her hair, she plucked the fabric of her dress off her skin and shook out the hem, droplets flying towards Farrell's trousers. He didn't notice, and they made no difference to how wet he was. His hair stuck to his head, and droplets of rain clung to his stubble and ran down his neck. Like her, his clothes were plastered to his muscled frame.

Thunder boomed outside, and the wind howled. This wasn't a storm; it was nature throwing a temper tantrum.

'I need to apologise for what I said to you earlier…but that can wait until we're dry.' He raked his hand through his hair, and water fell from his fingers. Thea looked at him and shivered. Before she could respond, Farrell swore and gripped her wrist. 'You're ice cold. Let's get you warm.'

Farrell led her up the free-standing staircase. His fingers provided a source of warmth she badly needed, and she wished she could lay her head against his chest and snuggle in. She was convinced he'd feel better than a hot shower and dry clothes. More fun too.

They squelched up the stairs, leaving puddles of water in their wake. At the top of the stairs, Farrell led her down a passage with tall, closed cupboard doors on either side. Beyond it was a bedroom, so she presumed this had to be the dressing room. Why did his guests need such a large dressing room for an island holiday? It seemed like a waste of space to her. She shrugged. Maybe his uber-wealthy guests required a dressing room the size of Madagascar.

Thea followed Farrell into an expansive bedroom. The wall behind the massive king-size bed was a deep navy, the colour echoed in the couch and armchair in the small sitting area to the left. The bed was covered by what she presumed was high-thread-count white cotton bedding and four plain, hefty pillows. A moody black and white seascape dominated the wall above the wooden headboard.

She didn't have time to take in much else before Farrell, still gripping her wrist, tugged her into the adjoining bathroom. It was spectacular—complete with a double-headed shower and a built-in seating area. A freestanding slipper bath stood near a wide picture window, and she instantly imagined the sea views from both bath and shower would be breathtaking. Oh, yes—she could definitely see herself stretched out in that tub, a cocktail or a glass of wine in hand, watching the sun sink behind the horizon.

Farrell released her hand to step inside the shower and flip on the taps. Almost instantly, steam started to billow, and her limbs began to defrost. 'Fresh towels are in the cabinet under the sink. Use the robe on the back of the door,' he instructed her, his voice curt. 'I'll open a bottle of wine. Or would you prefer something warm to drink? Coffee? Tea?'

Uh…? Why wasn't he leaving and venturing back out into the storm? This was her villa, right? Drinking wine with Farrell Wolfe? That wasn't something she'd ever imagined happening. And where was her luggage?

This was reputed to be a six-star lodge. 'My clothes haven't been unpacked and put away yet?' she asked, confused.

'Your luggage is still at the lodge,' he explained, his words terse. 'The storm caused some delays.'

Before she could think of a response, Farrell left the bathroom, closing the door behind him. Thunder rolled again, and Thea bit her bottom lip. Was it safe to shower during a tropical storm? Was she in any danger of being nailed by a lightning bolt?

Deciding to risk being fried to a crisp, as it was better than being cold, she stripped off her sodden dress, kicked off her shoes and removed her soaked underwear. Shivering, she walked into the monstrously big shower and tested the water, sighing with pleasure when she realised it was exactly the right temperature. Stepping under the hard spray, she turned her face up, loving the heat.

What a day, what an island and what an unusual welcome! But how did she feel about being around Farrell Wolfe? Confused? Worried? Attracted? Definitely.

The man was…seriously hot. He'd grown out of his 'pretty boy' stage and now looked more rugged, primal rather than perfect. Time had hardened him, made him more…inscrutable. Had it also made him kinder, or was his concern just an act? She'd certainly never expected him to apologise, let alone be so concerned about her being wet and cold. Then again, maybe she shouldn't read too much into that; she was a guest and was going to review his resort.

Had time changed her? She was still as independent as she used to be, as reserved. She still protected herself by observing life and not participating in it. It was, honestly, safer that way. And when she found herself craving the weight of strong arms around her, the scent of a man's skin, the steady rise and fall of a chest beneath her cheek—she reminded herself that company, and sex, were never worth the risk. A few years ago, she'd indulged in several one-night, one-week and one-month stands, but they'd all died a natural death. Mostly because she slammed on the brakes whenever she suspected unwelcome feelings had arrived, uninvited, to the party.

No, the real danger wasn't desire, it was intimacy…and the intense pain and resulting silence when it was whipped away. She remembered the seesaw of her childhood all too well, her parents dangling affection like a treat, then yanking it away the moment she reached for it. She'd never wanted to stop believing in people—but experience had taught her they would inevitably disappoint her. And she had no intention of living through that again. Honestly, living life solo was so much easier, less complicated and less…messy.

Thea reached for the shower gel and frowned at the contents on the shelf in the shower. An expensive brand of face wash and shower gel, specifically developed for men. She turned slowly and took in the electric razor on the counter between the his-and-hers sinks, the toothbrush and paste in a holder, and a hairbrush. There was a clothes hamper in the corner, and a pair of men's running shorts lay over the edge. A pair of expensive trainers, size twelve or thirteen, sat next to the door.

This wasn't a hotel bathroom, this was *Farrell's* bathroom. What the hell was she doing in his personal villa? Thea flipped off the taps and stepped out onto the big tiles. Bending over, she opened the cupboard under the sink and pulled out a large towel, gratefully wrapping it around her body. After towel-drying her hair, she eyed the robe on the back of the door, thinking she didn't have much choice but to put it on.

There was no way she was climbing back into her soaked dress and underwear.

Thea pulled on the robe, which promptly pooled at her feet, its sleeves dangling past her hands. Rolling back the cuffs, she cinched the belt as tightly as she could. She looked down at her hidden toes and at the cuffs, which kept unrolling over her hands. The thing was ridiculously big. What actually worried her, though, was the possibility of missing a step and pitching down the stairs—straight onto the polished concrete below.

She stepped out of the bathroom and eyed the oversized cupboard doors; she was sure she'd find a T-shirt or shirt of Farrell's she could wear that wasn't quite so dangerous. But rifling through his things felt too intimate, like crossing a dozen lines all at once. No, she'd make her way downstairs—carefully!—demand to know what the hell he was playing at and why she was in his private villa. Then she'd insist on being moved. Immediately.

Thea tossed her head, and wet strands slapped her cheek. She brushed them away and stepped towards the door.

First things first: don't die on the stairs.

CHAPTER THREE

Farrell heard her muttering as she made her way to the bottom level and transferred his attention from the wine bottle in his hand to the stairs on the other side of the room. His jaw slackened as he watched Thea tiptoe down, the robe he never used trailing behind her. He fought to hide his grin. She looked like a kid playing dress up, swallowed by the fabric. Her hair was swept back from her forehead, her make-up washed away by rain and the shower, and he found himself wondering when he'd last seen a woman who looked this stunning without any cosmetic help.

A spray of freckles peppered her nose and flowed onto her cheeks, pink from the heat of the shower. Her dark eyebrows and eyelashes highlighted her light eyes, and he caught a glimpse of her slim legs as the fabric of the robe parted as she walked. She looked exactly as he remembered her: defensive, closed off and more than a little annoyed.

'Why am I in your private villa?' she demanded, crossing the room to where he stood.

Right, she'd worked that out quicker than he'd imagined she would. Then again, the Thea he remembered had a razor-sharp brain. He pulled the cork from an excellent red and wondered how to answer her. He could lie, but that would come back to bite him on the ass, and, although she'd never believe it, he didn't like lying. His father had done too much of it, too often. He poured wine into two glasses, filling only the bottom inch of the glass. He offered one to her, and, when she glared at him, put it on the edge of the kitchen counter. He gestured to the barstool in front of her. 'Would you like to take a seat, or would you prefer to sit in the lounge?'

She eyed the stool and narrowed her eyes. Clutching the robe's belt, she awkwardly climbed onto it. Farrell clenched the stem of his wine glass, knowing that any offer to help would be instantly refused. The robe slid open halfway up her thigh, and his throat tightened, his stomach flipping. Good legs—no, great legs—and he loved her fire-red-tipped toes. A silver ring adorned the middle toe of her right foot, another fine chain circled her ankle, and…was that a tiny tattoo on the inside of her ankle? He forced himself not to bend down for a closer look.

Clearing his throat, he leaned his hip against

the freestanding island and sipped his wine, savouring its smooth glide, the hint of berries and rich oak. A branch clattered across the deck, bouncing off the glass. Not that he worried—every window and door in the resort was built to withstand tropical storms. Not quite bulletproof, but close. It was easier to think about the storm than her, and he latched onto the distraction.

It was worse than predicted and would batter the tiny island through the night and into the early morning. Branches would snap, sand scatter, leaves strip away—the meticulous gardens would take a hit. Definitely not the first impression he'd wanted to give VIP guests or the journalists. He just hoped they'd look past the mess tomorrow and trust his assurances that the staff would work overtime to restore the resort.

Storm clean-up was manageable. Handling Thea and her lack of a villa? Far less so.

'You still haven't answered my question,' she said, her tone frosty.

He'd get to that, but first things first. 'I apologise for my asinine comment earlier.' He swallowed his discomfort. *Just get it done, Wolfe.* 'Your presence caught me off guard.'

She tipped her head, her eyes drilling through him. Then she sighed and looked away. 'I was surprised to see you too,' she admitted. 'I didn't expect you to be here… I thought you had more important things to do.'

There was nothing more important to him than ensuring his developments lived up to every promise he'd made—to himself and to others. But he opted for the easy explanation. 'I like being on site, and, while I'm London-based, I can work remotely.' He sipped his wine and held the stem of the glass in a tight grip. 'Do you accept my apology?' he demanded.

Thea didn't hesitate. 'Yes. But I still want to know why I'm in your private villa.'

Right. That. He had no choice but to tell her the truth.

'Despite asking a guest whether he would be accompanied by his wife, and receiving a clear answer that he would not, he did, in fact, arrive with his wife…and his child.' Farrell opted for brevity. 'As a result, we are a room short.'

Thea raised an eyebrow. 'And I'm the one who lost out on the room?'

'Not deliberately, but it worked out that way. Ultimately, my only choice was to bring you here and hand over my bedroom to you. I'll sleep on the couch.' Actually, what he most wanted was to share his big bed with her—and not to sleep. Farrell bit the inside of his cheek, startled by the rogue thought. Twelve years ago, she hadn't been his type: too nervy, too intense, always making him feel guilty for who he was and the privileges he enjoyed. But this woman—with her wary eyes and tense, pushed-back shoulders—intrigued him. She was mysterious and remote, yet he'd glimpsed sparks in her gaze. He wanted to know whether it was a small flicker…or a raging wildfire.

'And why didn't you explain any of this to me before you shoved me onto a golf cart and drove me out into the rain?'

'The storm was quickly intensifying, and if I'd taken the time to fully explain then, we would've wasted time arguing, time we didn't have to get here safely.' As if to emphasise his point, an immense clap of thunder shook the villa. 'I simply decided to skip the argument.'

'You do know that you sound like an arrogant prat, right?' Thea asked, her tone surprisingly conversational.

He shrugged. 'Probably. But this was the solution that made the best sense.'

'So, the owner of the resort is going to give up his bed for a guest?' Thea asked, looking sceptical. 'Are the other guests going to buy that?'

He'd thought about that, too. 'I doubt they'd question it, or even care. If they ask, tell those who weren't there to hear it last time and remind those who were that we're university friends, and I invited you to stay at my private villa. They'll assume you are happily installed in my non-existent guest room.'

Thea tapped her finger against the rim of her glass. She'd yet to take a sip of the wine. 'But did you consider that my integrity as an impartial journalist might be compromised by letting everyone know that we're friends, by me staying in your villa? They won't believe I can be impartial.'

'And is being impartial so important to you?'

'My entire brand, my success, is based on my impartiality,' she whipped back, the fire he'd glimpsed flaring even brighter. 'My readers trust me because I always, always tell the truth.'

He made a point of never reading reviews, preferring to rely on his marketing and publicity teams for feedback. That she was here, on the island, and had been offered the chance to review his resort meant that she had some serious clout, but he hadn't realised how much. 'You could tell the world about our faux pas. I can't stop you. But I still don't have another option to accommodate you,' he informed her.

'Staff accommodation?' she asked.

He shook his head. 'I do have limited staff accommodation, but it's currently full because of the storm.'

Thea swore and looked out of the window, a frown pulling her eyebrows together. She was quiet for a few beats before picking up her glass and taking a sip. 'Nice,' she murmured.

It should be, it was a rare vintage and cost a fortune. 'So, I really don't have a choice but to stay here.' She turned those big eyes on him, cool and assessing. Then she wrinkled her nose. 'Ah, but how am I going to write about the guest accommodation if I don't experience it first-hand?'

That was easy to answer. 'The rest of the villas are modelled on this one,' he replied. 'I built it first, and the others are almost identical. Most of our VIPs are only staying for five days, and when they move on, you'll have another five days on your own in a villa.' He raised his own eyebrow. 'I trust that will be enough?'

Their eyes met, and the same electricity that powered the storm arced between them. She gave him a long, appraising look, and his skin tingled—in a way it never had before.

'Are you going to be okay sleeping on a couch?' she countered. 'You're big and tall. It's not going to be fun.'

He caught her little smirk, the amusement in her eyes. Oh, she was enjoying this—a little too much. She liked having him on the back foot. Probably because, back when they'd known each other, he'd done his best to keep her unbalanced, off kilter. Why? Because she'd made him feel too much, made him conscious of everything he was…and wasn't. He'd been a prick, yes, but he was a man who didn't let anyone—not even her—walk all over him.

'What if I suggest we share that enormous bed upstairs?' he asked, keeping his tone mild, non-threatening.

As expected, her cheeks flushed, and her eyes widened. 'What? Why would you ask that? *No!*' But when she pulled her bottom lip between her teeth and her gaze flicked to the bare skin at his collarbone—where his wet shirt had been swapped for a dry button-down—he knew exactly what she was thinking. She was attracted to him. She didn't want to be, but he was certain she was.

Had she always been? Or was it, like his attraction to her, something new?

She pointed a finger at him. 'No. That is *not* happening.'

There was a flicker of panic in her eyes, and he hated that he'd put it there. He lifted his hands, palms out. 'Thea, relax. You have my word: I'll stay on the couch,' he said, trying to soothe her.

Relief skittered across her face, so potent it tempted the devil in him. 'Of course, you might change your mind,' he added, voice teasing. 'Feel free to let me know if you do.'

Her eyes turned stormy, as wild as the one outside, and he knew it was time to change the subject. 'Are you hungry?' he asked. 'You didn't eat much at lunch.' He'd watched her pick at the meal—salads, seafood, freshly baked bread, and fruit. She was too thin.

Her eyes met his. 'You were watching me?'

'I watch every guest—it's literally my job.' To be fair, he employed people to do this for him, but he couldn't remember anything about the other guests—she was all he could recall from lunch. He was normally hyper-focused and detail-oriented, but Thea's arrival had blown apart his composure. What would living with her do? Shatter him completely?

'I am a bit hungry,' she admitted. 'I had a bit of a stomach ache earlier, that's why I didn't eat.'

He thought about what medicine he had on hand and thought he could, maybe, scrounge up some paracetamol. Would it help?

'Is it better now?' he asked.

'Yes, much.'

Thank God. He glanced at his fridge. 'I can offer you a charcuterie board, a cold lobster salad, and vichyssoise soup. Petit fours if you have a sweet tooth.'

Her eyebrows flew up. 'All that? Wow.'

'We knew a storm was coming in, and we weren't sure how bad it would be. As a precaution, Chef prepared a cold meal for our guests in case they couldn't make it back to the main dining room for dinner,' he explained. He glanced at the rain pummelling the window and nodded. 'It was a good call.'

Farrell sipped his wine before continuing. 'Predicting what Indian Ocean storms, any storms, will do is difficult. This one strengthened abruptly. We had no way of knowing that would happen.'

She glanced out of the window, tipped her head to the side and wrinkled her nose. Adorable. How could she be so sexy at the same time? It was a conundrum. He watched as she pulled the robe over her knees and rolled back the constantly unravelling cuffs. How was she going to eat while fighting the fabric? He could offer her a T-shirt to wear, but he doubted it would help.

'Do you want me to go fetch your luggage?' he asked. He'd get soaked again, but he'd raid the kitchen for some plastic garbage bags and protect her luggage from getting wet. As for him? Well, he had an entire wardrobe of dry clothes upstairs. Honestly, after all the pointed comments he'd sent her way when they were younger, it was the least he could do.

Thea stared at him for a few beats, and he thought she was biting the inside of her lip as she wrestled with the idea of sending him back out into the storm. Then her shoulders dropped, and she shook her head as she tugged at the cuffs of the robe. 'No, don't do that. It's wild out there. But I'd appreciate it if you could maybe lend me a T-shirt and a pair of track pants, something that's less…tent-like?'

He thought fast. His track pants, even those with a drawstring, would fall down her hips to puddle at her feet. But one of his dress shirts would adequately cover her, and if she pulled on a pair of his boxers and rolled them up, they might stay up. Or she could use the robe's tie as a makeshift belt. He made the suggestion, and she nodded.

Farrell placed his wine glass on the counter and straightened. 'I'll go dig something out, and while you're changing, I'll get supper on the table.'

'Thank you.'

She was still a woman of few words. Still mysterious, still made him feel on edge. When he was in his twenties, she'd been a threat to him, a threat to what he believed in—his standing, his privilege, his place in the world—and, yeah, to his intelligence. Now, his wariness was born of something bigger, scarier…a deep, undeniable attraction to a woman he shouldn't want.

But her and him—him and anything long-term or meaningful—were impossible. Wolfe wealth and ambition had decimated too many lives in too many places. The realisation that the wealth he'd once taken for granted—the fortune and company he'd inherited—had been built on stolen land and, possibly, a lost life cut deep, and left scars that wouldn't fade.

If he allowed Thea, or anyone, to look below the surface, she'd see just how unworthy he really was.

'Farrell?'

Thea calling his name cut through his thoughts and yanked him back to the present, his kitchen, and the storm howling outside. Right… he needed to go upstairs and find her something to wear. He pushed his hand through his hair and then ran it over his face. 'I'll leave the clothes on the bed for you.'

He crossed the room, climbed the stairs and tried not to imagine her hand in his as he led her up to his bedroom and into bed.

Because that wasn't something that would ever happen. Not with Thea Monroe.

She still looked ridiculous—Farrell's button-down shirt hit her thighs, and his boxer shorts were held up by the robe's belt—but she could, at least, use her hands. Thea hit the last step and—bam—darkness swallowed her whole as every light in the villa blinked out.

She heard Farrell's curse. 'Just stay still, Thea,' he commanded her. 'Don't move until I tell you to.'

Thea planted her bare feet on the floor, happy to obey. She didn't want to wander through an unfamiliar house when it was so dark she couldn't see her hand in front of her face. She was a city girl and knew she should be more scared than she was, but she wasn't, instinctively trusting Farrell to sort out the problem. Just ten seconds later, and after she heard some more creative cursing, the torch on his phone illuminated the space between him and her. 'Walk on over here, and take a seat,' he told her.

Thea walked across the room and took her same seat again. When he was certain she was settled, he turned away and started to rustle in the kitchen drawers. 'I could've sworn there were candles in one of these drawers,' he muttered. 'And why the hell didn't I remember to replace the inverter and battery pack?'

'Why didn't you?' Thea asked, placing her chin in her hand. 'Don't you have a PA, or many of them, to do your bidding?'

He looked at her over his shoulder, his eyes briefly going to her legs, before returning to her face. 'My personal needs are way down the priority list.'

'So, your house isn't hooked up to the resort

solar system?' Thea asked. It was one of the things that had intrigued her the most in their prospectus: they were promoting the resort as being as green as it possibly could be, with zero environmental impact, zero food waste, and using renewable energy.

'No, because my house is on the opposite side of the guest villas, and the working end of the resort. When I got the quote, it was exorbitant. Since I'm not here that often, I thought I could ride out the occasional storm and cloudy days.'

Farrell finally found some candles and slammed a drawer shut. In the flickering light from his phone, she caught his frustration. 'The guests are, and always will be, my priority. They will have power through the storm.'

'I won't,' Thea pointed out.

'You can't write about this,' Farrell replied, irritation in his voice. 'It's not a genuine guest experience.'

Thea wrinkled her nose. And that was the crux of it, wasn't it? Staying in Farrell's villa meant she wasn't having a true guest experience. How could she possibly know if what she was getting here was better—or worse—than what the other guests were dealing with?

Her being here wasn't realistic, not if she wanted to write a fair report. The only way to do that was to wait until she moved into a regular villa in five days. Then she could judge the space itself. Until then, her focus had to be on the resort as a whole—the amenities, the way it operated, its facilities and entertainment, the supposedly six-star food and service.

It was the only way to stay objective. The only way to be fair.

She watched Farrell shove the candles into the candle holders and light them. His face looked less harsh in the candlelight, younger too. Surprisingly, the gentle light stripped him of his easy charm and showed him to be a man with a great deal on his mind. Also, someone who looked a little exhausted.

Farrell placed a candle in the middle of the island, before switching off the light on his phone. Then he took her red wine away and placed a fresh glass in its place, a white wine glass, equally lovely, equally expensive. She watched as Farrell poured a light golden wine into her glass. 'Why?' she asked. 'I was perfectly happy with the red.'

Farrell shook his head. 'This wine pairs well with the lobster and the soup. The red wine doesn't.'

He wiped the wine bottle with a napkin and placed it on the counter, in the corner, out of the way. Thea looked down and took in the perfectly set table, the cutlery in straight lines, the linen napkin with sharp creases. There was another wine glass, this one containing water, perfectly aligned with the plate setting. She was dressed in his clothes, with no make-up on, bare feet, but the table setting was immaculate. Clearly, you could take the boy out of the hotel, but not the hotel out of the boy.

Farrell placed her lobster salad in front of her.

It looked like something that belonged in a gallery, not on a plate—too beautiful to touch, let alone eat. This was what they served in a storm? *Seriously?* But if it tasted half as good as it looked, she was about to be ruined for lobster salads in the future.

Farrell sat opposite her, a gorgeous man in a suddenly too romantic, too dramatic setting. This felt surreal, a bit weird, and more than a little overwhelming. She didn't know how to act—like a well-respected travel blogger with a huge following? Or like someone who had known him when he was, frankly, awful? Or as a guest simply grateful to be out of her wet clothes and to have somewhere safe to sleep out of the storm?

She rubbed her forehead and stared down at her plate. 'This looks…amazing. Thank you.'

Farrell stood, half leaned over the island, and, with the concentration scientists used to split the atom, drizzled a vinaigrette over her food, before rubbing away a tiny drop from the rim of her plate with his napkin. Reaching over, Thea placed her hand on his, feeling the raised veins of his hand and trying to ignore the sparks skittering up her arm. 'Farrell, stop.'

His eyes met hers, and one eyebrow lifted. 'What?'

'This isn't your resort's dining room and I don't need a perfectly presented plate of food,' she told him. Pulling her hand back took more effort than she imagined, and she was surprised to see her fingers trembling. Dropping her hand to her lap, she tried to smile. 'Look, it's been a long day for me, and, I imagine, for you. Can we just drink the wine, dig into the food and call a truce for tonight? You don't have to impress me, and I don't have to act like a journalist reviewing the resort.'

His strong hand gripped the napkin, bunching it in his fist. He held her eyes for a while and finally nodded. 'Okay, we can do that,' he said, pulling out his chair and sitting down. He topped up his wine glass, took a healthy sip and closed his eyes. When he opened them, he looked at her. He gestured to the candle and sighed. 'No electricity, no villa, no luggage. It hasn't been a good start.'

He didn't like failing, didn't like being on the back foot. And she could understand that, as he was reputed to be driven, someone who demanded perfection.

'Booking mix-ups happen, and you can't control a storm. I'll judge the resort on what I experience when I move into a villa.' She smiled at him. 'I'm going to have a little holiday, at your expense and in your house, until then.' She lifted some salad to her mouth, chewed and sighed. It was delicious. 'So why don't we put today on the back burner and start again in the morning?'

He nodded, picked up his fork, and speared a chunk of lobster, lifting it to his mouth. Dear heaven. That mouth. It was indecently sexy—so tempting. Heat shimmied through her, sharp and inconvenient, and she grabbed her water glass, tossing it back as if it were tequila. Food first, she told herself, then bed. Tomorrow she'd wake up, and maybe—if the universe was feeling generous—her life would make a fraction more sense.

CHAPTER FOUR

THE NEXT DAY, Thea stepped out onto the wide wooden deck and sucked in a sharp breath. Oh, wow. Below her, a private cove curved, its white-gold sand disappearing into transparent water that shifted from one shade of blue to another. On either side of the beach, more enormous granite boulders jutted from the sea, smooth and glinting silver in the sun. The waves rolled against the rocks, early morning lazy, and, far out beyond the cove, the horizon shimmered in molten blue. To her left and right, palm fronds stirred, their battering at the hands of the storm last night already forgotten.

She liked Petit Saphir. No, she might even be in love. It was tropical-island perfect.

When she'd stepped out of the bedroom this morning, she'd found her suitcase outside the door and immediately lugged it inside and flipped it open. Hoping she'd be at the beach sometime soon, she pulled on her prettiest swimsuit, a mint-green and white check bikini. Over it she tied a matching sarong and, because she didn't want to burn, a gauzy white top. After slathering her face with factor five-thousand sunblock, she opted to wear waterproof mascara and gloss on her lips, knowing that the humidity would wipe any make-up off later in the day.

She heard footsteps on the deck behind her and turned. Farrell, dressed in a navy button-down and black board shorts, skirted the outdoor furniture and handed her a steaming mug of coffee. 'Morning.' He pushed the cup into her hand, his smile crooked. 'How did you sleep?'

She'd had to untangle herself from his overly large shirt, but after she'd shucked the shirt and boxers and slid between his sheets naked, she'd passed out, despite the noise of the raging storm. But if she mentioned sleeping naked, she'd blush, and he might think she'd spent some time wondering what it would be like to share his bed with him, equally naked.

She had, but he didn't need to know that.

She sipped her coffee, keeping her eyes down. 'Good, thanks,' she told him. She glanced into the lounge behind him. The doors that were a barrier between them and the storm had disappeared, sliding into the walls of the villa, and his lounge and deck were one open space. Lovely. His pillow still lay on the longest of the couches. 'How did you sleep?'

'Not too bad.'

Thea was pretty sure that was a lie. He looked tired; the lines next to his mouth were deeper this morning, the smudges under his eyes darker. 'Be truthful—did you get any sleep at all?' she demanded.

He lifted one shoulder. 'I'm not a great sleeper at the best of times,' he admitted. 'I got an hour or two.'

She grimaced. While she was, sort of, on a mini holiday, Farrell was working. Apart from entertaining his VIPs and guests, he also had an international company to run. The man needed sleep.

'I'll sleep on the couch, you can take the bed,' she impulsively told him.

'Not going to happen,' Farrell replied, his tone and expression resolute. 'You're staying exactly where you are.'

He tried to smother his yawn, and Thea wrinkled her nose. While it wasn't her fault that she didn't have her own room or villa, she did feel bad that the owner of the resort had to sacrifice his bed for her. She somehow knew arguing would be useless. 'It's a stunning day,' she commented. She gestured to the view with her cup. 'It's hard to believe we had such a violent storm last night.'

Farrell placed his back to the view and crossed

one ankle over the other. 'I did an inspection of the island and resort this morning,' he told her, his tone conversational.

Thea rested her forearms on the railing and turned her head to look at him. His scent was an intriguing mixture of the sea and citrus, and something exotic and spicy. 'And was there much damage?' she asked, interested.

'The resort held up well,' he said, obviously pleased. 'It's one thing to design buildings to withstand storms, it's another to know they will.'

Thea took a sip of her coffee. 'When we flew in, the pilot buzzed another island, which looked reasonably close to this one. Was it damaged at all?'

Farrell shook his head. 'I checked in on them as well. Like Petit Saphir, they only had minor damage, which is a miracle, given the intensity of the storm.' His smile strengthened. 'But, best of all, while I was out, I saw a Seychelles Paradise Flycatcher.'

She grinned at his enthusiasm. She would never have pegged him as a bird guy. 'And that's good, I presume?'

'It's amazing! It's a bird native to La Digue— the Seychelles' third most populated island,' Farrell explained. 'The thing is, all the development there is chewing up its habitat. To help the population, they've moved some breeding pairs to Denis Island and here. Neither island has mammal predators, so the birds actually stand a chance.'

She slowly straightened, surprised by his words. 'I know that this is a green resort and self-sustainable, but I didn't realise that you, personally, were this passionate about the environment.' She grimaced. 'Not that I should… It's just not something that's reported on.'

He didn't speak, and Thea asked a follow-up question. 'Have you always liked nature?'

His eyes met hers, cool and a little distant. 'What do you think?'

He looked as if he could handle a little honesty. 'No. When I knew you, I didn't think you cared for anything but yourself.'

He mimed pulling the trigger on an imaginary gun. 'Bingo.'

Colour her intrigued. 'When did that change?'

'When I took control of the company.'

Mm, that was the truth, but not, she decided, the whole truth. Then Farrell's expression turned cynical.

'Don't get too excited, I would never have developed this island if it wasn't viable,' Farrell explained. 'Building out here, especially when you use environmentally friendly products, is massively expensive. Then you need to hire the right people to build the resort, and asking them to work on an undeveloped island means paying them well over the going rate. Then there's the transport costs.'

'So why did you do it?' Thea asked, fascinated by this glimpse into his psyche. She'd never, not once, thought that Farrell would be an eco-warrior who gave a damn about the environment.

'Because I can charge the big bucks to make it profitable.'

She held his gaze, silently demanding more. He sighed and looked away. 'If I hadn't bought this island, someone else would have—and they'd care a hell of a lot less about the environment than I do. They'd build a massive resort that made a fortune but wiped out the sea life in the process. There's a turtle-nesting beach on the far side—a place that's perfect for swimming, for water sports—and another developer would've sacrificed the turtles to entertain their guests. There's even a waterfall and a natural pool, and I know someone would've slapped a swim-up bar there and called it paradise.'

He shuddered and, in that moment, Thea knew he cared more about the island than even he was prepared to admit.

'If you care so much about it, then could you not buy it and leave it as it is?' Thea asked, still gripped by this side of Farrell she'd never imagined existed.

Farrell snorted. 'I wish. It was eye-wateringly expensive, and my shareholders would never have approved of the purchase without the promise of a decent return. Also, the sale agreement stated that the island had to be developed for tourism, providing local people with jobs. A resort was the best way I could balance the two.'

He seemed so different from the money-hungry and status-obsessed Farrell she remembered. That young man hadn't seemed to care about what was right or wrong, about anything outside the privileged and wealthy bubble he'd occupied.

They said that people didn't change, but had he? Really? Was it possible for people to do a one-eighty, or was she just hoping to see something that wasn't there? That was what she used to do as a child. She'd latch onto a slight change in her parents' attitude—a nice gesture, some kind words—and start imagining they'd changed. But a heartbeat later, they'd revert to being the self-involved monsters they were. Change never lasted long.

She couldn't forget that Farrell needed to impress her, to impress all the journalists he'd invited to his resort. Their opinion wouldn't make or break him, but it would determine if the resort broke even sooner rather than later. They weren't powerful enough to draw people to the resort in droves or to make them boycott it, but they had some influence. Farrell knew that environmental issues and sustainability were massively important to her. Was he simply telling her what she wanted to hear? Was she being too cynical? Maybe. But then life had taught her to be.

'I'm not the same person you knew back then,' he quietly stated. 'And I apologise for every horrible thing I ever said to you.'

Wow. Now, that was unexpected. And so damn sincere. What else could she do but accept his apology? 'Thank you,' she said. 'I appreciate that.'

He nodded. 'It's twelve years overdue. I'm also sorry about the mix-up in your accommodation,' Thea,' Farrell added. 'I know it hasn't made a great first impression on you.'

He sounded tired, stressed, and uncomfortable. Three emotions she'd never expected to see on his face or hear in his voice. But, really, how much did it matter? She'd had a great meal and slept well, and it was a stunning day.

The next few days would be packed—meals in the dining room, long hours wandering the resort—so she wouldn't be under Farrell's feet. He'd be busy, too, running his empire and charming his guests, which meant their paths would cross only over a quick coffee in the morning, if that.

And honestly? Staying in his villa wasn't exactly a hardship. It had that luxurious, castaway-on-a-private-island vibe, the kind of place that made her forget the rest of the world existed. Things could've been worse. They *had* been worse.

'It's a pretty, pretty day, Farrell,' she quietly said, 'and I'm not sleeping in a shack. Besides, I'm not the one sleeping on the couch.' She tipped her head to the side, taking in his long, wide frame. 'Be honest, how was it? Awful?'

His little wince told him everything she needed to know. He was too long and too wide. 'Had we been better friends at uni, I would've invited you to share your monstrously sized bed; it's big enough to sleep four,' she joked. Dear God, where had those words come from? Their eyes slammed together with all the force and heat of a meteor strike. On the big screen in her mind, she watched a montage of his moves: him, shirtless, arm muscles bulging, his hands on either side of her head, looking down at her with desire in his eyes. Her lifting her face, needing his mouth on hers, desperate to know how he tasted, or whether his ever-present stubble would scrape her skin, or if it was softer than it appeared. Her legs would open, waiting for him to settle between her thighs, his erection nestling…

Wow! What the hell?

Thea pulled in a deep breath, fire creeping

up her neck and into her cheeks. She released a short, huffy breath and dropped her head, and made a big deal of looking at her watch.

'So, I'd better go get breakfast…um, your staff have arranged water sports in the bay, jet-skiing, paragliding, paddleboarding…with instructors,' she gabbled, her words as fast as bullets. 'I need to eat breakfast, I'm a monster without food, and I need to find my sunblock.'

Dear God, she needed him to say something, anything. Biting her lip and praying she wouldn't see the smirk she remembered on his face, the arrogance and entitlement in his eyes—*I'm a Wolfe, and gorgeous. Rich, too!*—she forced herself to meet his gaze.

She caught a hint of confusion, awareness, and an acceptance of whatever was dancing between them, but no expectation, no arrogance. What would he say about her asinine comment about sharing the bed? How would he respond?

'The beach activities only start at ten-thirty, or whenever someone makes it to the beach. My staff work to the guests' timetable, not the other way around, so go when you are ready. Have you done any of the activities before?'

She latched onto his change of subject, so grateful he'd done so. 'I've tried paddleboarding, the other two things, no,' she said. 'But I kept falling off the paddleboard, as my balance is terrible. I might just sit on the beach and watch.'

Farrell twisted the masculine silver and leather bracelet he wore on his right wrist; it half covered his well-worn vintage Rolex. 'Would you be interested in doing something different?' he asked.

While she never minded sitting on the beach under an umbrella with a cocktail in her hand and a good book to read, she wasn't opposed to an adventure. This older, sharper-edged, but nicer version of Farrell intrigued her. She wanted more time with him—purely, she told herself firmly, to measure just how much he'd changed. Nothing more.

'What do you have in mind?' she asked.

'We've been rehabilitating a reef on the north side of the island, and I've been working with marine biologists from the Seychelles and South Africa. I'm joining them to help plant coral babies.'

She blinked, not sure she'd heard him right. 'I'm sorry, what?'

'We're trying to reseed a reef.' He folded his arms and grinned. 'It means spending the morning on a boat, but you can snorkel over the reef, it's pretty in some places. The last time we went out, we ran into a pod of bottlenose dolphins and hung out with them for an hour or so.'

Sitting on the beach doing nothing versus watching scientists doing their thing to rehab a reef? As she was a huge promoter of the environment, there was no way that she was going to miss watching Farrell in action. But why was she being singled out to witness what would be a huge selling point in his favour? The other journalists should know about this, too.

'Are you going to take your other guests and crew to see the reef at another time?' she asked, rocking from foot to foot. 'I'm sure they'd like to see it.'

Farrell looked past her shoulder to a spot out to sea. After a long few seconds, he shook his head. 'This isn't something I'm promoting, and I don't want you to write about it, either.'

That made no sense at all. 'I don't understand. Why wouldn't you want anyone to know about what you're doing?' she asked, genuinely confused. It would gain him great PR points.

His expression turned stubborn. 'You can come if you agree that this is off the record. Besides, you're on holiday for the next few days.'

'I don't understand why—'

Farrell interrupted her. 'I'm already running late, so you need to decide. Yes or no?'

She didn't want to miss out on what promised to be an amazing adventure, so she nodded her head. She'd take mental notes and talk to Farrell about his reluctance to include such a newsworthy endeavour in her reporting later. Judging by his mulish expression, there was no point in trying to persuade him now.

'I'm definitely coming,' she told him. But because she thought she should warn him about her incoming arguments, she pointed her index finger at his wide-as-Canada chest. 'But we will argue about this later.'

The side of his mouth hitched in a small smile. 'I'm sure we will,' he told her, gesturing inside. 'Hat, bikini, sunblock, Red.'

Red, the nickname he used to call her back in the day. She waited for irritation to bite, for annoyance to wash over her, but this time it didn't.

Strange. Then again, so much of this Seychelles trip was turning out that way—unexpected, offbeat…surprisingly good.

The boat was almost too beautiful, Thea thought, as the sleek white vessel sliced through the sea. Despite its polished teak decks, chrome, and daybeds, today it looked less like a billionaire's toy and more like a working vessel.

Only Farrell could turn scuba-diving into a six-star experience.

But the real surprise wasn't the elegance—it was the chaos. The deck where she sat was cluttered with crates of coral fragments, mesh frames, and marine biologists, some wearing short wetsuits peeled down to their waists, some not, discussing a recently rediscovered fish species. Their chatter was quick, efficient, and jargon heavy. There was also an urgency to them, a subtle suggestion they weren't here on some vanity project. That this was science. Real, urgent, important.

Somehow, the gloss and the grit worked together—Farrell's yacht buzzed with hope and the vague notion that substance could be sexy, too.

Talking about sexy... Farrell stood at the wheel, the wind blowing his hair back as he expertly handled the big boat, his eyes hidden behind expensive sunglasses. He'd escorted her on board, introduced her around and, from her seat, she'd watched as the yacht's skipper had stepped aside for him, handing over control of the vessel. His movements were fluid and experienced, completely confident. Sometime between the villa and the boat, a couple of buttons on his shirt had opened, and the fabric fluttered in the wind, revealing his tanned chest and ridged stomach. He wore no shoes, and even his big feet were sexy.

He looked like a modern-day pirate, someone very at home on the ocean, under the bright African sky.

Farrell decelerated, the boat slowed, and then he cut the engines. As the boat came to a rocking stop, the marine biologists, three women and two men, reached for their dive equipment. Farrell lowered the anchor and made his way over to Thea, dropping to his haunches in front of her. He gestured to a buoyancy vest and an air tank in the well behind her. 'I'm going to go down with them, give them a hand. We'll all be on nitro; it saves us time if we use air. The reef isn't deep, so if you want to snorkel above us, you'll be able to see us work.'

Thea lifted her hands in confusion. 'I still don't understand what you are doing,' she said.

He pointed at the plastic crates filled with water. 'So, artificial reefs can be created using eco-safe concrete structures or stone. Lots of places have used sunken boats to create reefs because fish like structure, they need something to hang around, and coral needs something to attach to.'

'I heard that sailors don't often catch fish in the mid-oceans, because fish don't like open water,' Thea said.

He rocked his hand back and forth. 'There might be some truth to that. Anyway, getting back to what we're doing today...' He rested his forearm on his knee and pushed his hair back with long fingers. 'Basically, we are going to seed the coral. We'll take coral fragments, these guys call them coral nubbins, that have been harvested from healthy reefs in the area—'

'Actually, the majority of these were grown in our lab,' a perky blonde—who, as Thea had noticed, couldn't take her eyes off Farrell—interrupted him. Thea gritted her teeth, self-aware enough to know she was a teeny-tiny bit jealous of her curvaceous body, surfer-blonde hair and her bright blue eyes. She was a baby marine biologist, not far into her degree, and Thea hoped Farrell considered her far too young for him. Because she was…

Farrell's eyes didn't leave Thea's face. 'Thanks, Jane,' he replied. Thea caught his minuscule eye roll, and she had to swallow her grin. 'As I was saying, the nubbins are either transplanted from healthy reefs or grown in underwater "coral nurseries" and then attached to the artificial structures with eco-friendly glue or ties.'

'And this works?' Thea asked, impressed.

Farrell nodded. He stood up and reached past her to pick up his mask and fins. Casually dropping them into her lap, he shrugged off his shirt and laid it on her shoulder. Amused by him using her as a clothes hanger, Thea watched as he picked up a buoyancy vest from the well and rested it at her feet.

'Duck,' he told her. Thea bent her head, and Farrell reached over her and effortlessly lifted a tank from behind her, which he placed next to her knee. Around them, the divers suited up, going through their checks, helped by the resort staff. Farrell waved off help from his employee and connected the tank to the buoyancy vest. He then connected the air supply and checked the air flow to the regulator. She looked around, wondering why he wasn't suiting up in the empty spaces on either side of her.

'Do you want me to move?' she asked, wondering if she was getting in his way.

Farrell looked at her, his eyes reflecting amusement and more than a hint of heat. 'No, I like being near you,' he softly said, his voice a little deeper, a little more growly.

What…was she supposed to say to that? And why did she feel the same? As if everything was a little brighter and better whenever he was around. She shook her head, confused. This was Farrell, her uni nemesis, the pain in her arse, the entitled rich kid, who was insufferable and sometimes cruel.

Farrell gripped her chin lightly. 'Look at me, Thea.'

She lifted her eyes and took in his masculine face, his intense expression. 'Are you the same person you were twelve years ago?' he asked.

She shook her head. Of course, she wasn't. She wasn't as insecure, was calmer, less uptight. 'No,' she admitted.

'Me neither,' he said. Her breath caught when the pad of his thumb skirted briefly, too briefly, over her bottom lip, before his hand dropped. 'Can you remember that?'

She touched the top of her lip with her tongue, then nodded. 'Yes,' she whispered.

Farrell nodded, then reached for his mask and fins and tucked them under his arm. He gestured to where the marine biologists were standing on the dive platform, ready to climb down the ladder to slide into the bright blue, lake-flat ocean. 'The head biologist wants to do a briefing, so I should go listen.' He called for his skipper, who immediately hustled across the boat to stand at Farrell's side, his expression deferential. 'This is Jean-Pierre, Thea, and he'll get you your snorkelling equipment. The water is warm; as you can see, I don't bother with a wetsuit, but you might want one. JP will keep an eye on you when you're in the water, but don't go too far from the boat.'

Thea nodded.

'If you dive down to the reef to get a closer look, don't touch anything, okay? Apart from it being dangerous, rockfish have excellent camouflage, and your fingers can kill the coral, even if you are gentle.'

She wouldn't be diving, so that wouldn't be a problem.

'As I said, we'll be on nitrogen, so we'll probably be down for ninety minutes, maybe a little longer,' Farrell continued. 'It's shallow, so we can stay down for a while. You'll be okay for that long?'

Of course she would, she assured him. Farrell nodded, and, waving off JP's offer to carry his tank and vest, smiled at her. 'I'll see you in a bit. Ask JP for whatever you want to drink.'

He seemed reluctant to leave her—sweet but confusing—so Thea waved him away. 'I'm fine, go. You've got a reef to save, Wolfe.'

He smiled and, in that moment, he looked years younger. 'Yeah, I do.'

Thea watched him as he walked away, swallowing her appreciative sigh. Jane made room for him at the dive platform, and Thea relaxed when Farrell ignored her coquettish smile. She'd never expected Farrell Wolfe to be so involved in an ecotourism project, to care so much. Why did he want to keep his involvement secret?

Who was Farrell Wolfe? He wasn't the young man she remembered, nor was he the ambitious CEO determined to dominate the luxury sector of the tourism market. Who was he really, beneath that exceptionally good-looking package? And why did she now suspect he was deeper, more interesting, more complicated—far kinder—than she'd ever imagined?

CHAPTER FIVE

FARRELL PAUSED WITH a fist-sized lump of coral in his gloved hand, the lukewarm saltwater pressing against his skin, the world muted but for the thrum of his own heartbeat. There was a special type of silence below the sea's surface, akin to an empty, history-soaked cathedral. Above him, Thea sliced through the water as if she belonged there, long legs scissoring, hair fanning out in a reddish cloud against the sunlit surface. Light fractured around her, turning her into something unearthly, unreachable. She'd only arrived less than eighteen hours ago, but it felt as though she'd been around him longer, for months, even years. In the water, on the boat, in his home, and, terrifyingly, in his life, she didn't destroy his internal rhythm…she felt right.

Rocked by his rogue thoughts and looking for a mental reset, Farrell cleared his mask, took a hit of nitro and forced his attention back to the reef. But his hands felt clumsy now, his chest too tight.

He kicked his legs gently to fight the slight current, perfectly buoyant as he hovered over the reef. He quickly attached the nubbin and tested the tie, happy when it didn't move. Being in the ocean, doing this, made him feel useful, as if he were rebalancing some cosmic scale. It was easy to donate his boat to the cause, the fuel, his staff, and fund the foundation that grew the coral, the people who did the research, but there was something special about getting your hands dirty. Or, in his case, wet.

He'd been to the Seychelles more times than he could count, drifting through expensive resorts, playing on chartered yachts and ski-boats. In his teens and early twenties, he hadn't given a damn about the ocean—or the people who lived with it, off it. Why would he? He'd been arrogant enough to believe the world bent to his will.

But one memory still had its hooks in him. He'd been sixteen, maybe seventeen, on a so-called boys' trip with his dad and his cronies. His father, showing off, had hired a gleaming boat and insisted on being the skipper. They'd fished, snorkelled, and laughed too loudly. And when it was time to leave, his dad had shoved the throttles forward, forgetting—or not bothering—to pull up the anchor.

He could still see it now. The reef falling apart as the anchor tore a long, brutal gouge into the living coral. His father had doubled over laughing, his friends slapping him on the back, as if he'd provided them with some entertainment. And Farrell had laughed too.

He'd forgotten about the incident until he'd been forced to face the numerous similar, but exponentially bigger, actions his father had taken in his quest for profit. But the destruction of the reef still haunted him, as did the faces of the Seychellois crew, their shock, their grief—they'd looked as if someone had died in front of them. But he'd shrugged it off, and demanded food, a drink, as if their pain, the ocean's pain, had meant nothing to him. Why should it? His father hadn't given a damn, so why should he?

The shame of it still burned.

Thea had had every right to despise him back then; in fact, she'd been more tolerant of his behaviour than he'd deserved. He'd resented and despised people who stood for something—especially sharp, uncompromising people like Thea who saw through his polish. He'd wielded privilege like a weapon, and his casual cruelty had left scars.

He'd spent years trying to atone for his and his father's sins, but how much would ever be enough? Would there ever be a time or place when he felt he'd done enough, where he could stop looking over his shoulder and breathe? If there was, it still felt years, possibly decades, away.

Farrell looked at the reef, smiled at an aqua and yellow nudibranch, no bigger than the tip of his thumb, his thoughts far away, his breathing the only sound.

He glanced up at Thea, admiring her starfish pose, legs and arms akimbo, gently bobbing in the water, her expression under her mask a little blissful. She was gorgeous, ten times more attractive than the gawky, earnest young woman he remembered.

And, God, when she'd made that comment about sharing his bed, it had taken every bit of willpower he had not to crush her mouth beneath his, sweep her up and haul her up the stairs and lay her on his bed. He wanted her, and he was experienced enough to know that she wanted him, too.

But—*crap*. He couldn't go there. Couldn't even think about exploring the heat between them. He needed her to write a fair, honest assessment of the resort—to show that he wasn't just spouting BS about sustainability. He didn't want her—or anyone—to gush about the reef rehabilitation project; after everything Wolfe International had done, taking credit for something so small felt wrong. But he did want her, and the other journalists, to see that he was genuinely trying to do better.

Getting emotionally—or, worse, physically—involved with Thea was a recipe for disaster. And if he did, it would quickly end: a few nights, then done. Because he didn't believe in more than that. Couldn't.

If anyone ever bothered to look past the polished charm and easy smiles, they'd see the truth—that, underneath, he was hollow, eaten up by guilt. Unworthy. Back then, Thea had had the uncanny ability to see straight through him, and he suspected she still possessed it.

So, no. He'd stay on the couch. Keep his distance.

If he could.

Happy to bob, Farrell waited for the biologists to leave the ocean, his staff hauling vests and tanks up onto the boat with ease and familiarity. After the last of the divers climbed aboard his boat, he swam over to the ladder and unclipped his buoyancy vest and slipped it off his body. Holding it, as it was still attached to his tank, he waited for JP to reach down before pushing the vest and tank up and out of the water. JP swung it onto the deck, and Farrell gripped the bottom rung of the ladder, about to climb onto the boat.

He looked up to see Thea sitting on the top step, a bottle of icy water in her hand.

She rocked it from side to side, silently asking if he wanted it. Hooking his elbow around the ladder's last rung, he caught it when she dropped it, cracked it open it and took a long swallow. As the chilled water slid down his throat, he looked up at her, taking in her slim body, his cap covering her hair and her upper half covered by a long-sleeved rash vest protecting her pale skin from the high-in-the-sky sun.

He gestured to the ocean behind him. 'What do you think?' he asked.

She looked down at him, her grey eyes warm, tinged blue from the reflection of the ocean. She offered him a huge smile, the first he'd seen that was spontaneous and completely natural. 'It's… wow, it's amazing, Farrell. I don't know much, but I can see the impact. There are parts of the reef that look like they are growing.'

Yes, they'd done good work down below. And it felt good. Even better to have Thea sitting on his boat, smiling down at him. He took in her pink cheeks, the hint of sweat at her temples. 'You look hot. Why don't you come in for a while?'

She looked behind her to where the rest of the team were milling about, either drinking water or stripping off their suits. 'Don't you want to get going?' she asked. 'I'm sure you have so much to do back at the lodge.'

He did, but it could wait half an hour or an hour. He was about to answer when he caught movement out of the corner of his eye. A sleek dark shadow blocked out the reef below. 'Thea, come down the steps now and slip into the water, quietly.'

Her eyes widened. 'Why?' she asked.

'You'll see.'

Thea edged her way down the steps and dropped into the water, next to him. Farrell released a high-pitched whistle, and JP popped his head over the side. 'We've got a whale shark under the boat,' he said. 'Tell the others to come in quietly. We don't want to scare it off.' He tossed his water bottle to JP, who caught it one-handed.

Thea's hand curled around his forearm, her nails digging into his skin. He looked at her and saw the fear in her eyes and winced. She reached for the ladder to haul herself out of the water as quickly as possible, her face petrified. Farrell reacted fast, wrapping an arm around her waist and hauling her back against him, and her shoulder blades hit his chest and her bottom his groin. She fitted into him like a puzzle piece he hadn't known was missing.

'A whale shark is a fish, not a shark, and is

completely harmless; it's just big. It eats krill, and you are of no interest to it at all.'

Some of the tension went out of her body, and she placed her hand on his wrist. 'Are you sure?' she asked.

'I've been diving these waters since I was a kid, Thea. I'm very sure that, as deliciously pretty as you are, the whale shark will not consider you a snack.' He felt himself hardening and sighed. He couldn't say the same for himself. He wanted to touch and taste her…everywhere. Knowing that she would soon clock his arousal, if she hadn't already, Farrell released her and put some distance between them. Thea gripped the ladder and he trod water, quietly asking JP to toss them two masks and snorkels. He caught them, handed Thea one, and quickly pulled his mask on, duck-diving deep to see where the fish was and hoping it hadn't moved off.

It was swimming away, somewhat lazily, and Farrell cursed, thinking they'd lost their chance to see the amazing forty-foot creature up close. He was about to surface when it suddenly did a right-hand turn, gracefully turning its huge body to return to the boat, as if curious about what he was and what they were doing. Surfacing next to Thea, he saw that her mask and snorkel were on, and, as the others slipped into the water, he took her hand and led her away from the boat. He pointed out the whale shark—although it was hard to miss—and locked his eyes on Thea, taking in her huge eyes and shocked expression. She placed her hand on her chest, obviously entranced by the massive fish. It had slowed down, seeming interested in the strange creatures in his watery world.

Thea's hand tightened around his, and he smiled. He'd never realised this when he was younger, but now he knew there was something incredibly special about these interactions with nature, these experiences that couldn't be replicated. Any one of them could die, or be seriously hurt, by one swish of the huge tail, but Farrell knew it wouldn't happen. There was no danger here, just inquisitiveness and, strangely, respect. And humanity. He felt far safer in the Indian Ocean than he did in corporate boardrooms on dry land.

There was no nonsense here, there were no lies, no tactics and strategy. No guilt, no deceit...

Just the warm, stunningly clear ocean. And Thea.

Right now, in this moment, it was all he needed.

Thea walked down the path to the outside entertainment area next to the swim-up bar. Some of the guests were in the pool, some were seated at the outside bar, and others were milling around the fire pit. Some, like her, were dressed for dinner. She rubbed her stomach; she was starving and looking forward to the seafood buffet they'd been promised.

Thea touched her hair, a little self-conscious. On press trips like this, she stayed in the background and rarely interacted with the fellow guests, partly because she was shy, and partly because she never felt she fitted into their 'I write for a prestigious travel magazine' clique. They all had bylines, were well known in the industry, all veterans of travel writing. She was simply a blogger who, through honesty and transparency, had managed to gain a significant following. Her writing wasn't flowery or nuanced; it was simple, direct and desperately honest.

Despite the fact that her readership far exceeded the others', she still felt as if she didn't belong. Then again, when did she ever? She'd never felt at home with her parents and she'd been so different from the other students at uni—working, supporting herself and being a fully-fledged adult—that she didn't understand them. Or they her.

But this morning, in the water, her hand in Farrell's, she'd felt relaxed, as though she belonged, her hand feeling right in his. A crazy idea because Farrell Wolfe was the last person she could see herself with. He wasn't her type of person—too slick, too charming, too charismatic. His polish and confidence made her chest tighten; she wanted to believe he'd changed, but experience whispered that no one ever really did.

Although, he'd shown her a different side of his personality this morning. Away from the lodge, he'd been relaxed and direct, honest and involved, his eyes sparkling. It was obvious he enjoyed the process of rehabilitating the reef. He'd listened to the head biologist, his attitude respectful, and had given his staff calm, clear orders, with a grateful smile and an occasional joke. He'd ignored Jane's flirting, and he'd paid a lot of attention to Thea…

God help her, she'd loved it. It had made her feel fluttery and flustered, horribly off balance but in the best way. Really, looking at the man, all ripped muscles under tanned skin, hair mussed by the wind, white teeth flashing, hadn't been a hardship either. He looked like a surfer, a dive instructor, hot and hard and sexy…someone completely in tune with the wind and the waves.

Desperately, possibly fatally, attractive.

Which was why she'd paid a lot more attention to her looks tonight than she normally did. On returning from her unexpected adventure, she'd driven a golf cart back to Farrell's villa. When she'd caught a glimpse of herself in the bathroom mirror, she'd grimaced. Her hair had been a tangled mess of curls, she'd lost all her make-up, and she'd counted new freckles on her nose and cheeks. Her face had been a little red from sun or wind burn, her eyes bloodshot from the saltwater. She'd looked as young as she had when she'd first enrolled in uni...

After an afternoon nap, she'd showered and washed, dried and curled her hair into soft waves. She knew that trying to cover her freckles was impossible, so she'd rubbed a tinted moisturiser on her face and darkened her eyelashes with heaps of mascara. Lip gloss and a fitted, pretty sundress, with flat sandals, completed her summer-evening-at-a-tropical-resort look. She hoped Farrell liked what she was wearing—

She shouldn't care what he thought, shouldn't even be thinking of him as a man, like that. She knew she was looking for trouble and would soon find it. She'd grown up with people who changed their attitudes at the flip of a switch, so she couldn't risk trusting the changes she saw in Farrell. She'd been let down too many times before, had shed too many tears. It was easier to expect the worst than be disappointed. And when she looked at Farrell—at all that charm and polish—a warning dinged: trust him, and you'll regret it.

'You look so pretty.'

Thea turned slowly at the sound of his deep voice, her heart banging against her ribcage. Farrell had shed his surfer-boy image from earlier and now looked like the rich owner of the resort. He wore lightweight summer trousers in a pale blue, cropped at the ankles, and expensive loafers without socks. A navy open button-down with rolled-up cuffs covered a white T-shirt, and an expensive watch, this one a sleek number, encircled his wrist. He'd slicked back his hair but hadn't bothered to shave. Yet again, Thea willed herself not to test the softness of the stubble on his chin and jaw.

'Hi,' she whispered, caught off guard by the wave of attraction to this man who'd whipped back into her life.

He stepped closer to her, and she inhaled his scent. She wanted to plant her nose into his skin, on that spot just below his ear, and breathe him in. She mentally shook her head, thinking that this tropical island was getting to her…

Farrell's thumb grazed her cheek. 'You caught some sun today,' he commented, his deep voice raising goosebumps on her skin.

'I get freckles at the first hint of sun,' she replied, a little bereft when his hand dropped down to his side. 'The curse of the redhead.'

His eyes flickered to her hair, and he smiled. 'I like your hair; when the light catches it, it's the colour of the sun as it slips beneath the horizon and night takes over.'

How on earth was she supposed to be professional when he said things like that? 'Thank you?' she said, wincing at the uncertainty she heard in her voice.

The corners of his mouth tipped up. 'That was a compliment, Thea.'

Um, okay. The thing was, she'd received so few of them, she didn't know how to respond when she was handed one. Rocking on her feet, she gestured to the outside bar. 'I could murder a drink,' she told him, desperate to get moving. Because if she didn't, there was a good chance that she'd fling her arms around his neck and kiss him stupid.

She looked at his mouth and quickly dropped her gaze. *Get behind me, temptation.*

Farrell placed his hand on her back, his touch light, and they walked towards the bar, framed by strings of twinkling fairy lights. Farrell greeted the guests sitting at the bar and asked her what she wanted. After he'd placed the order, he pulled up a barstool for Thea and helped her onto it. Thea noticed his eyes lingered on her bare legs a little longer than they should. Then he turned to his other guests and asked about their day.

They effusively answered him, raving about

the water sports, their stunning day on the beach, and how they'd buzzed about the bay on jet skis. But Thea knew she'd had a far more meaningful, far nicer day. She could paddleboard and jet-ski whenever she wanted, but swimming with a huge whale shark and watching a reef being rehabilitated? Those were rare, and wonderful, will-always-remember-this-day experiences.

It was such a pity she couldn't write about them, but when they'd docked, Farrell had reiterated his request for everything to remain off the record.

'We didn't see you on the beach, Thea,' Gwen, a legendary writer for one of the world's most recognisable travel magazines, commented. 'But I suppose that, as a redhead, you tend to avoid being outside.'

She made her sound like someone who was allergic to the sun. Thea sent her a cool smile. 'I had a lovely day, thank you.'

Gwen's pencil-thin eyebrows rose. 'Doing what?'

'This and that,' Thea blandly replied, and took her margarita from the bartender with a smile.

'I suppose you were running around the island gathering research for your blog,' Gwen stated, her tone slightly waspish.

Thea tipped her head to the side and swallowed her sigh. Yep, there it was, she was being patronised. It wasn't the first time Thea had felt like a bug beneath designer heels.

Behind Gwen, her companion grimaced and sent Thea an apologetic smile. She lifted her shoulder in an infinitesimal shrug. She'd heard it all before. But when were the OG journalists like Gwen going to realise that people had moved on, that they consumed most of their information online? That magazines were dying? Nobody her age had bought a magazine in for ever, and she'd bet that Gwen's articles got more reads online than from physical copies.

'Now, Thea, darling, where did you study journalism?' Gwen asked, her lips around a pink straw, highlighting the lines from decades of smoking. 'Or did you just hit it lucky?'

The witch. 'I graduated with a degree in journalism from LSE,' she replied, keeping her voice even. Living with her parents had taught her to never show her irritation or frustration, especially not anger or hurt. Emotions were weapons that could be used against you.

'Thea and I were in the same year,' Farrell interjected. 'She was an amazing student. I always knew she was going to be an excellent journalist.'

Gwen narrowed her eyes. 'But can you call what she does journalism?' she asked, her smile venomous.

Thea started to respond, but Farrell's grip on her shoulder told her to keep quiet. 'Thea has more than ten million subscribers on all platforms, and many of them are hardcore travel enthusiasts. Interestingly, her subscribers range from the ultra-wealthy to backpackers—'

Gwen released a high-pitched trill, nails-on-a-chalkboard unpleasant. 'I doubt backpackers would be interested in any articles on Petit Saphir,' she scoffed.

His grip tightened fractionally. Was he annoyed? 'Backpackers consider places like this aspirational, a resort they can see themselves visiting in the future, on their honeymoon or when they retire. Thea's articles plant seeds for people who can't afford to visit here now but might be able to later.' He looked at Thea, his lips curving into a smile. 'Do you follow her on social media, Gwen? Her feed is amazing.'

He lightly tapped his beer bottle against the rim of her glass. 'I especially liked the series you did on Chile. When my life settles down, I'd like to take some time to visit the places you suggested.'

How she'd love to show him the unique stilt houses and wooden churches of Chiloé Island, and amble around the town of the port city of Valparaíso with him. To introduce him to sopaipillas off a street-food truck in Santiago. She could see them there, together. *God.* What was wrong with her? She'd never been able to imagine anyone sharing her travels before.

A resort staffer walked up to Farrell, and he turned away to speak to him, his beer bottle in his hand. Thea liked that he was prepared to drink from the bottle, that he wasn't so uptight to insist on a glass. She sucked on her perfectly tart, perfectly zingy margarita and released a low hum. A gorgeous man was being attentive, the night was warm, she was about to eat fantastic food, and she could feel the pleasant buzz from her cocktail. Okay, she could do without Gwen, but what could she do about that?

Farrell turned back to her and, once again, placed the tips of his fingers on her back. She turned at his touch, and her eyes slammed into his. His fingers extended, and his entire hand spanned her back, warm and solid. Heat and want, lust and need shot through her and all the moisture in her mouth disappeared. She wanted this man. In the most carnal way possible.

Judging by the heat flaring in his eyes, he wanted her too.

They were sharing a villa, with only one bed. Maybe they could, possibly…

Farrell's hand dropped away, and he stepped back, his face suddenly expressionless and unreadable. Thea fumbled for her margarita, and in the process the glass wobbled and the liquid splashed onto her hand. Farrell reacted by asking the barman for a serviette, and he wiped her hand. 'Shall we join the others for supper?' he asked, his expression now stoic.

Thea tugged her hand from his. 'That sounds good,' she chirped, wincing at the hints of panic and confusion in her voice. She hopped off her chair and, leaving her half-drunk margarita behind, walked towards the long, beautifully decorated table.

She needed a glass of water, a mountain of food, and a chance to find her equilibrium. And her self-preservation. Because once she was fed and watered, she could think clearly. And when she did, she'd come to the only sensible conclusion that a—what? A one-night stand? A fling? A dalliance?—with Farrell would be spectacularly unprofessional and downright dangerous.

Dangerous to her objectivity. Not to mention to her heart.

Because Farrell wasn't just any guy. He was the one who, years ago, had irritated her, infuriated her, pushed every single one of her buttons. And now? Now he intrigued her. Made her want to look closer, peel back layers to see who he'd become…and how much more there was to find.

She wasn't one to take risks, to colour outside the lines. But how she badly wanted to.

CHAPTER SIX

IT WAS DANGEROUS to walk on a sandy beach on a tropical island under a full moon, but when Farrell asked whether she wanted to walk off supper, Thea quickly agreed. Barefoot, she trailed Farrell down the wooden steps from his villa, following the narrow path winding towards the private cove below his house. The moon was so bright a torch wasn't needed. They stepped onto the sand, but Farrell surprised her by leading her through a small gap between two massive boulders, and out onto a wide, empty beach. For a moment, it felt as if they were the last two people on the island—maybe in the world.

She tipped her face up to look at the moon, silver and stunning. 'It's just so beautiful,' she quietly murmured as the sea rolled over her feet, warm and silky smooth.

'Isn't it?' Farrell agreed, sliding his hands into the pockets of his trousers.

'Will your guests have access to this beach?'

she asked, smiling at a tiny crab scuttling across the sand.

He shook his head. 'No, I think I'll keep this one to myself. Besides, this is where the turtles nest, and I don't want them disturbed.'

She didn't blame him; she wouldn't let anyone else onto this beach either. She loved this ecologically aware side of Farrell. 'When did you first discover this island?' she asked.

He looked at her, his expression inscrutable as moonlight highlighted his rugged face.

'I must've been eight or ten the first time I came here,' he said, eyes on the horizon. 'My dad had hired a yacht, and we'd return every summer, exploring the islands one by one. This spot… It's always been one of my favourites in the whole archipelago.'

'Then you grew up and bought it.'

'Yes,' Farrell replied.

She cocked her head, sensing that there was a huge story behind that single word. She wanted to push him for more, but sensed his retreat, just like a crab returning to its shell when threatened. She hated intrusive questions herself, so she pushed back her curiosity.

'I'm sorry about Gwen,' he said after they walked a few more yards.

Thea shrugged. 'I've heard worse.'

'How did you get to be one of the biggest in

dependent voices for travel on social media?' he asked.

She smiled. 'I was working at a now-defunct online women's magazine, and they asked me to go to Greece. I was tasked to write an article on travelling solo as a single woman. I wrote the article, but I also threw up a couple of videos on the various platforms, not thinking anything of them. I thought they'd be a good way to preserve my memories of the trip, because I didn't know when next I'd get to travel.'

'And your editor loved what you did,' Farrell said, his white teeth flashing as he smiled.

'He did, and he sent me on another trip, to Morocco. I did the same thing, got more views, got great feedback.' Thea stared at the ribbons of light cast down by the moon onto the sea. It looked like an AI image, something generated after a 'give me a picture of a moonlit beach at night' prompt. Too pretty to be real.

'Two weeks after that, the magazine closed and I was out of a job,' she explained. Should she tell him how scared she'd been, that she'd pounded the streets looking for another job, only to find nothing? That when she'd run out of her savings, she'd sold all her stuff, packed a rucksack and bought an air ticket to Thailand, thinking she'd find work teaching English? 'I went travelling and ended up doing more videos, more blog posts. I found a way to monetise them, and the rest…'

'Is history,' Farrell finished her sentence for her. His eyes met hers, and Thea felt unsettled. Why did it feel as if he could see straight into her soul?

'Why do I feel like you left out vast swathes of that story, and that it wasn't as easy as you make it sound?' he asked.

Because it hadn't been. Because there had been months when she'd barely managed to feed herself or afford somewhere to stay. She'd taught English in Japan to make money and packed fish in Norway. Worked as a nanny in Singapore. But she'd kept plugging away, making videos, honing her craft, writing blog posts, digging out the lost or forgotten delights of a city. And she'd gained a loyal following, which had started to grow by word of mouth…

'Because it wasn't,' she admitted. 'But I'm in a good place now.'

He gripped her wrist, lifted it and ran his thumb over the Cartier tennis bracelet she'd bought herself as a Christmas present last year. 'I can see that. Good for you.'

'A lover could've bought it for me,' she pointed out.

He shook his head. 'You wouldn't accept such an expensive gift from a lover unless you were very serious about him, and you're single.' He squinted at her. 'You are single, right?'

'I am,' she confirmed. 'But I could've accepted the bracelet from a man I had a fling with.'

His mouth curved into a smile. 'Thea, you wouldn't even accept cups of coffee from your fellow students back in the day. I doubt you've changed so much that you'd accept a very expensive tennis diamond bracelet now.'

She grimaced, remembering how she'd questioned everyone's motives, never understanding that a cup of coffee could simply be a cup of coffee. 'I was pretty spiky,' she admitted.

Farrell rubbed the back of his neck. 'I never wondered why, nor thought about what might have shaped you. I am curious now, though.'

She felt his eyes on her, but she kept her gaze on the sand, on the surf curling in and out. If she looked at him, saw that quiet interest, she might spill secrets she'd never voiced to anyone. Strange, really—of all the people she'd met in twelve years, Farrell Wolfe was the one tempting her to open up.

Was attraction—simple chemistry—muddying her thinking? That would be the rational explanation. And yet beneath it, deep and stubborn, was a sense she could trust him, that he wasn't the man he'd been before. But that was exactly the kind of wishful thinking she'd applied to her parents, and, time after time, they'd proved her wrong.

Could she afford to make the same mistake with Farrell? No. Definitely not.

She folded her arms and pulled up a shaky smile. 'It's a beautiful night, but it's been a long day, and maybe we should head back.'

Before I do something really stupid, like grab your shirt, stand on my tiptoes and plaster my mouth on yours.

Farrell nodded, turned, and they started retracing their steps back towards the boulders and the path leading up to the villa and the big bed she was occupying alone. Thea sighed. She'd had a few lovers before, but it had been a while, and she missed resting her cheek on a hard chest, falling asleep with the sound of a masculine heart beating under her ear, a heavy hand on her hip.

She also missed sex.

She was pretty sure that if she suggested a one-night stand with Farrell, or a fling for as long as she was on the island, he'd take her up on her offer. She'd seen the heat in his eyes, the hunger on his face, the way he frequently looked at her mouth, her legs, her chest. She wasn't offended by him checking her out; she did the same to him whenever she had the opportunity.

'What has you thinking so hard, Thea?' Farrell asked gently.

She risked looking at him and lifted one shoulder, prepared to lie her butt off. 'Nothing much,' she breezily told him, grateful when he didn't push her for more.

Farrell walked onto the deck and stopped at the open sliding door, the low lights of his lounge beckoning her to enter. The night seemed stiller now, and, for some reason, it felt as if the world were holding its breath. Even the crickets and the sea seemed quieter, as if waiting for the punchline of a joke. As she was about to step inside, his strong hand on her forearm stopped her. Thea braked, looked up into his face, and gasped at the naked need on it. His hand slid down her arm, and he linked his fingers with hers, his touch sure. Swallowing, she held his gaze, wondering if he'd close the slight gap between them and kiss her. She hoped he would.

She couldn't wait another minute to know what Farrell tasted like, to find out if being in his arms was as devastatingly wonderful as she'd started to imagine.

Then Farrell bent down and his mouth brushed hers once, a whisper of contact that felt more like a question than a kiss. Thea's pulse tripped, her body already answering before her mind could catch up. Her fingers fisted in his shirt, the fabric tight between her knuckles as she gave a quick, desperate nod—praying he'd read it for what it was: her kiss-me-more yes. He deepened their kiss slowly, deliberately, as if he wanted her to feel every shift of his lips, every flicker of heat. She tasted whiskey and chocolate on his tongue, but underneath both was the unmistakable taste of Farrell—somehow familiar but also dangerously new.

Her fingers curled into his shoulders, holding on, because the ground had tilted beneath her feet. He kissed her as if he meant it, as if he had all the time in the world, as if there were nothing beyond this moment. And she kissed him back, knowing she should pull away but incapable of doing anything but wanting more.

Then, just when her body was melting into his, Farrell stepped back. The night air rushed between them, filling the spaces he'd just heated, and Thea felt stripped bare, trembling. Her lips still tingled, her breath caught somewhere between her throat and her lungs. She hated how much she already missed the weight of his mouth on hers, how his retreat left her aching.

'What is it?' she asked, her voice croaky.

'I want you,' he stated, his tone rough. 'I want to walk you up to my room, lay you on my bed, and love you until the sun comes up.'

Direct. In your face. Clean. She appreciated

him being all three. She opened her mouth to agree—he was single, she was single, they were allowed—but the words wouldn't roll off her tongue. Uncertain and confused by her conflicting emotions, she pulled her hand from his and stepped back.

Farrell lowered his hands and slid them into the pockets of his trousers. His expression turned guarded. 'I thought we were on the same page,' he said, more formal now. 'I'm sorry for misreading the situation.'

Oh, that was BS, and he knew it. What had happened to his honesty from earlier? 'You know you didn't misread anything, Farrell!' she snapped. 'You're perfectly aware that I am attracted to you as you seem to be to me.'

He frowned. 'Then what's the problem?' he asked. He lifted his big shoulders in a quick shrug. 'We could have some fun.'

She did not doubt that Farrell knew his way around a woman's body and that she'd be on the receiving end of concentrated pleasure. But she couldn't say yes. Couldn't make her lips form the word when every instinct screamed that she needed to be cautious. Self-preservation, her old friend, sat heavy in her chest, tangled with fear. Farrell wasn't the type of man you could sleep with and forget. His memory would linger on;

he'd haunt her long after he walked away. And that was exactly why she hesitated.

But there was one reason she could give him, one he couldn't argue away. A truth, but not the whole truth. 'Farrell, I'm writing a story on your resort—on you, to some extent. If we sleep together, I risk my objectivity. And that's something I can't afford to lose.'

His hot gaze seared through her, and she prayed he wouldn't try and convince her, mostly because she knew she might be persuaded to dive in headfirst.

Farrell finally nodded, then sighed. 'Fair enough,' he calmly stated. Then he tipped his head to the side and sent her that half-smile that made her ovaries quiver. 'For the record, I think we're both mature enough to separate our attraction from work, our feelings from what you need to do. So let me know if you change your mind.'

She shouldn't. She couldn't.

She didn't think.

Knowing there was nothing left to say—and that with every second that passed she risked throwing herself against his chest and caution to the wind—Thea slipped inside and headed for the stairs. It was going to be a long night.

And maybe every night after this would be longer still.

* * *

After showering and changing into a pair of sleeping shorts, Farrell stretched out on the longer of the two couches in his lounge and watched the night sky off the deck. He'd left the sliding doors open, hoping a breeze would pick up off the ocean and cool down his heated skin. He placed his forearm over his eyes, trying to remember when he'd last felt this frustrated, when he'd last lain awake thinking about a woman he couldn't have.

He sank deeper into the couch, letting the night swallow him, eyes fixed on the stars. Her refusal gnawed at him. Oh, he'd been rejected before; he wasn't a sexual god, but Thea's refusal felt bigger and bolder, a cannonball straight through the barriers he'd built to prevent him from becoming emotionally attached and then hurt. He hated that he couldn't switch off his desire for her, that she'd made him feel unsteady, raw in places no one ever saw. This was exactly why he'd always avoided relationships—he feared letting someone in, was terrified of anything he couldn't control, scared that wanting her would bruise him.

Farrell stayed there, staring at the glittering sky, the quiet of the villa pressing in around him. Part of him wanted to pull himself together, to lock this longing away where it couldn't hurt.

But another part—louder, relentless—refused. Every memory of her touch, every glance, every teasing half-smile replayed in his mind. He wanted more. Of everything.

Was this more than simply sex? Unfortunately…because he sensed it had the potential to be more than a quick affair. And he knew the risks. Letting her in meant exposing himself, allowing her to see the man behind the wealth, the control, the public persona. But the ache in his chest and his groin, the mixture of desire and fear, wasn't something he could switch off. He wanted her—needed her—more than he had the right to, and that truth was both terrifying and undeniable.

And it scared him more than anything ever had.

It was day four on the island—and in Farrell's house—and as Thea headed down the steps to the living area, she gave herself the same morning pep talk as she had yesterday: act natural. Keep your smile cool, your emotions contained, and—most importantly—stay out of touching distance.

She was here to write a story on the resort, to observe, to take notes, to report on what she found. She might not write for the world's best travel magazines, but she was as professional as

Gwen and the other journalists who'd been invited to this island.

She wouldn't compromise her ethics.

But, good grief, how was she supposed to keep her distance when Farrell stood in the kitchen dressed in just a pair of black sleeping shorts, his wide, tanned back rippling with muscle? His hair was mussed, and the material of his shorts clung to his perfect bum…

Oh, she was in so much trouble. Thea was about to return to his bedroom—she couldn't cope with a half-naked Farrell—but he spun around, and his eyes slammed into hers.

Thea stopped, the world dissolving as her gaze landed on him. Farrell leaned against the counter, every muscle, every line of his body radiating heat, and his eyes locked on hers with an intensity that stole her breath. Desire flickered across his face, darkening his eyes—raw, unapologetic, impossible to ignore—and it hit her like a physical force. Her pulse hammered, a rush of heat crawled up her neck and landed between her legs, and the space between them crackled, charged, dangerous.

'We can't, Farrell,' she told him, lifting her hand. There was no point in pretending she didn't want him, and his excitement, outlined by his shorts, told her she was wanted too. Very much so. 'I have to keep objective.'

He gripped the edge of his counter, his knuckles turning white. 'Write whatever the hell you want,' he told her, his voice two octaves deeper than its normal growl. 'But get your arse over here and kiss me.'

She shouldn't, of course, she shouldn't, but she'd never seen a man look at her with such need, green eyes glowing, lust dancing in his eyes and across his face. It made her feel feminine and powerful and…yes, *wanted*. Needed. Being wanted like this—utterly, wholly—was her kryptonite, something she couldn't fight. Unable to resist any longer, she ran to him, flinging herself at him. Farrell, thank God, reacted quickly and hauled her up and into him. Somehow, by their own volition, her legs wound around his hips, her arms around his neck and her mouth landed on his lips.

But instead of falling into a soul and inhibition-destroying kiss, they both slammed on the brakes, as if needing to delay the anticipation, just a little. His lips were firm and a little chapped from spending time in the sun, and she smelled mint on his breath. Needing to know, she lifted her hand to his jaw, her thumb rubbing his stubble. Soft, she thought. Much softer than she'd imagined.

'I can't wait to kiss you again, Thea.'

There was only one first time, only one moment when it could be exactly this—charged, trembling, brand-new. The anticipation pulsed through her like electricity, slow, steady and exquisite, and she realised that holding back, waiting, made everything sharper, more alive. Every brush of his hand, every look that lingered too long, stoked the heat between them. She wanted him, wanted them, but she also wanted this moment to be right, in every way.

Still holding his jaw, she traced the seam of his lips with her tongue, sliding past his teeth. She felt him shudder, and his hand under her bottom tightened; the one on her back pulled her closer so that her breasts pushed into his chest. It was a light kiss, but her nipples tightened and her core throbbed. Yeah, she suspected they were about to blow the roof off.

'Thea,' Farrell murmured. She heard her name coming from a place far away, but then he took control of their kiss, his tongue plunging into her mouth, twisting around hers in a dance that was as old as time. Thea hung on, it was all she could do as he explored her mouth, changing the angle to go deeper, to kiss her harder. Thea was vaguely aware of him walking, and then she felt a wall behind her, and Farrell's hard body pushing into hers, his erection rocking against her panties as her hiked-up dress fell across the top of her thighs. He wrenched his mouth away and kissed her cheek, trailed his tongue along her jaw, and bit down gently on the lobe of her ear.

'You are so sexy,' he growled, dipping his head to kiss her neck, her collarbone, the ball of her bare shoulder. 'And you smell so good. I spent all last night, and the night before, thinking about this, thinking about you.'

Thea dropped her head back, sighing when Farrell's hand covered her breast, his thumb instinctively finding her nipple and rubbing it into a hard, tight point. A ribbon of fire connected her breast to her womb and set every nerve alight. She could no longer feel, she was simply sensation. Her entire world had narrowed to this place and time, this moment. Nothing mattered any more, she simply needed Farrell to keep kissing and touching her.

She'd never felt this way before, needy and lovely, desperate and excited. 'Say you want me, Thea,' he softly ordered her, his eyes boring into hers. She had more chance of pushing the earth off its axis than walking away from him now. Oh, a part of her, the sensible, rational part of her, knew this was a mistake, that she was entering too deep waters, but she didn't care. He made her feel alive, more alive than she had in years. It was a precious gift...

Thea placed her hand on his chest, her fingers drifting through the light hair on his pecs.

So hard, so warm. She pushed her nose into his skin, inhaling his woodsy, sexy scent, part deodorant, part hot man, and sighed. She was doing this; there was no backtracking now.

Farrell swiped his thumb over her bottom lip. 'Having you in my arms is everything, Thea. You're so tempting,' he said.

'Be tempted, Farrell.' Was that really her voice? Low, soft, her words coated with desire? She placed her open mouth on his collarbone, and her tongue slid over his skin.

She wanted him. She'd never wanted anyone as much as she did him. 'Make love to me, Farrell.'

Thea heard his relieved sigh, and his hand moved to her lower back. He pulled her closer to him, and her stomach connected with his erection, hard and thick. He bent his knees and his eyes, hot and needy, slammed into hers. 'I might lose my mind if I don't have you under me in ten seconds flat.'

His mouth covered hers in a kiss that stopped her synapses from firing. It was hot, wet, warm, desperate. Thea wound her arms around his back and pressed her breasts into his bare chest, needing to push past his skin and muscles, to find herself in the heart of him. Her tongue tangled with his as their kiss turned desperate and demanding.

His hands slid up the backs of her legs and onto her bare butt cheeks. He pulled away from her, his eyes fever bright as his hands danced over her scarlet thong. 'I don't think such a little amount of fabric can be classified as underwear,' he said, his voice hoarse. He stared at her, his fingers kneading the bare skin of her bottom. 'I thoroughly approve. I love thongs, the sexiest underwear ever. You are full of surprises, Thea.'

She hooked one arm around his neck as he pulled her dress up to her waist, the heat of his hand a contrast to the cooler air swirling around her bare thighs and bottom. 'I like that I can surprise you, Farrell.'

Farrell handed her a deep, wet, demanding kiss, and she gripped his thick hair as he plundered her mouth. He approached sex as he did everything else, with complete confidence and skill. Her nipples pebbled, and the space between her legs ached.

He pulled back to look at her, his eyes a stunning shade of green. He pushed his erection into her, somehow managing to connect with the neediest part of her. 'I want you. Can you feel how much? Let's head upstairs, sweetheart.'

Thea was struck by the faint trace of disbelief in his voice, as if he couldn't quite believe his luck. And as Farrell carried her up the stairs, she couldn't believe he hadn't realised that, right now, she'd follow him anywhere.

Without question, and without hesitation.

CHAPTER SEVEN

In Farrell's bedroom sunlight spilled through the open doors that led onto his balcony, painting the space in golden morning sunlight.

Farrell turned, smiled at her and held out his hand, and she slid her much smaller hand into his. His fingers tightened, and heat shot up her arm. She stood close to him and had to tip her head back to look up at him. His eyes darted from her mouth to her eyes and back again.

'I've wanted to kiss you from the moment you stepped out of that plane,' he told her. He cradled her cheek in his palm and rubbed his thumb on the arch of her eyebrow. 'You are beautiful.'

She waved his words away. 'Pfft. I skipped down the stairs earlier in search of coffee and didn't bother with make-up. I'm not even wearing mascara,' she told him. His eyes darted over her face, taking in her unpainted mouth and the freckles on her nose and across her cheeks.

'Let me amend that...*very* beautiful, in fact.'

Feeling lovely, Thea placed her hands on his

chest, her palms searing his skin. He lowered his head, and his lips brushed hers, cool, firm, sexy. He nibbled her bottom lip, and Thea went up on her toes, wanting more, desire heating her skin. She brushed her lips against his, her tongue dipping into his open mouth. He banded an arm around her lower back and easily lifted her.

He tasted of mint and madness, was warm and wild. Thea's legs encircled his hips, and she rocked against him, wiggling to get closer. Yeah, this.

She'd never felt this way before. Invigorated, turned on and sexy, as well as safe. Farrell, this reticent man, knew exactly how to touch her, what she wanted, how she wanted him. Thea arched her neck and sighed when his teeth scraped over the cords of her neck, when his lips drifted over her collarbone. Trusting that he'd hold her, Thea crossed her arms over her chest and lifted her dress and slowly pulled the material over her head. She dropped it to the floor, keeping her eyes on his. Her bra followed her dress to the floor. His eyes were now dark, more black than green, as they scanned her breasts. She briefly wished they were bigger, fuller.

'You're perfect,' Farrell murmured, alleviating her insecurities with a sexy growl. He lowered his head and pulled her nipple into his mouth, scraping his teeth over its sensitive flesh. So damn good. He switched to her other breast, and Thea tipped her head back, floating on sensation.

But, as much as she loved his attention, she needed to touch him, too, to give him as much pleasure as he was giving her. Thea slid down his body and, when her feet hit the floor, she brushed her hands over his chest, over his ridged stomach and knocked his hand away from the band of his shorts. Farrell sucked in a deep breath when her fingers stroked over his erection. She smiled, enjoying the effect she had on him. Wanting to tease him, she ran her thumbnail from the tip down, loving the sound of his harsh breathing. Pushing her fingers under the band of his sleeping shorts—designer, naturally—she slid them down his legs.

Farrell sat down on the edge of the bed and looked up at her with burning eyes. 'Stand between my legs,' he ordered her, his voice rough with need. Thea did as he asked, and he skimmed his hands up her sides, over her stomach. His thumb skated across her already hard nipples, and she moved closer, needing his lips on her. She needed his lips everywhere. Thea speared her fingers into his soft hair, loving the way he trailed his mouth across her skin, flirted with her nipples before pulling them against the roof of his mouth. She was already completely turned on, and she wanted him now, inside her, filling her, completing her.

'I haven't been able to stop thinking about you, about this,' he muttered, when his mouth moved to her ribs, his lips streaking over her skin. She clasped his face in her hands, forcing him to look up at her. She couldn't believe eyes could be that intense, that a man could look so fierce when making love. As if she were someone to be conquered, made to submit…

Instead of freaking her out, the prospect excited her. Only Farrell could make her feel this way.

Farrell pulled Thea onto his lap. Her thighs straddled his, and he yanked her close, and when her core hit his hard, hot shaft, they both shuddered. Farrell lifted his hips to grind against her, and Thea saw stars behind her eyes. If he kept doing that, she'd come…right now.

Realising she was on the edge, Farrell slowed down, his mouth skimming her shoulders, his hands running up and down her back, over her bare backside. Her hands did the same, taking in as much of him as she could, loving the muscles in his back, the bumps of his spine, the slight scratch of his chest hair against her breasts. Farrell lifted his mouth, covered hers, and his tongue explored her mouth in a lazy, lovely kiss. The heat was there, but banked now.

It just needed one spark for it to roar into a blazing inferno.

Farrell, using just one arm and a whole lot of core strength, picked her up and laid her on her back on the bed. He stood between her legs and dragged his fingers down her body, skating over the scarlet fabric covering her folds and skimming over her core. Thea moaned and lifted her lips. 'Farrell, take them off, please,' she pleaded.

Farrell shook his head. 'I rather like them on,' he told her.

Farrell stroked her again, all thoughts of her underwear obliterated. Thea sucked in a harsh breath when Farrell dropped to his knees and pushed her legs apart, and his clever tongue stroked her through the fabric of her panties, causing her to lift her hips and whimper.

'Please, Farrell.' She wasn't the type to beg, but she wanted what only he could give her, as quickly as possible.

Farrell's satisfied chuckles warmed her skin, and he used one finger to pull her panties to the side, and he slid another finger inside her, his thumb resting on her core. Ribbons of colour and intensity blew through her, and she managed, just, to demand he kiss her. Farrell sucked her into his mouth as he worked another finger into her, stretching her. But it wasn't enough, she needed him, all of him...

Thea sat up on her elbows, and her ragged breathing filled the room. 'Farrell, come inside me, please. I need you.'

He looked up at her, his face tense, and nodded once before looming over her, his tip probing her entrance. He muttered a curse and pulled back.

'What?' Why wasn't he inside her? What was he waiting for?

'Condom,' Farrell muttered, scrabbling in his bedside drawer.

'Hurry,' Thea told him, her hands stroking over his back, his sides, down his stomach and fisting him. He groaned and jerked against her. After sliding on the condom, he sent her a long look before picking a strand of hair off her face and tucking it behind her ear. 'Are you sure about this, Thea?'

God, *yes*. Utterly. 'Very. I want you, so much.'

She lifted her hips and shuddered when he positioned himself at her entrance. Farrell's eyes held hers and, although he didn't speak, she caught the longing on his face, knew how hard it was for him to slow things down, to make sure they were on the same page, reading from the same book. 'Make love to me now, Farrell. Please.'

Farrell slid inside her and buried himself deep within her, and Thea gasped, feeling herself stretch to take all of him. In tune with her, he stopped and raised his eyebrows. 'Okay?' he demanded.

'Very.'

Thea closed her eyes as sensations, tinged with pinks and blues and yellows, rolled over and through her, every wave lifting her higher. 'No, look at me, Thea. I want to watch you as you come,' Farrell demanded.

She looked at him through half-closed eyes, thinking he looked like a warrior, his face a study in concentration. He was waiting for her, and only after she found her release would he let loose and fly. She wanted to see him lose control, just once. She wanted to see him when his defences were down, when he was not in control. Using all her strength, she rolled him onto his back and dragged her core across him, before pulling him back and slipping her hips down. She groaned as Farrell gripped her hips, biting his bottom lip in concentration.

She was so close, but she wanted him wild and free; she wanted to watch him lose his mind. She lifted herself up, slid down slowly and then clenched her internal muscles. His eyes widened and his mouth dropped open as he struggled to hold onto his orgasm. She repeated the motion, and he groaned. 'Thea, I can't, please...you've got to...'

She liked him insensible, liked him like this. He was usually so controlled, a little buttoned down. She rocked again, squeezed again and told him to let go. Farrell tried to hold on, but then he sighed and bucked his hips, driving up into her, pounding her. She found his rhythm, and her climax built with all the speed of a bullet train. She saw him grimace as his fingertips dug into her hips, and his face ended up in her neck as she felt, deep down inside her, his release. And as he fell apart, she followed…falling, tumbling, spinning…

After a trip through time and space, after being turned inside out, she landed in his arms, against his neck, safe and in the place she most wanted to be.

Much, much later, while lying on Farrell's chest, Thea stroked her hand up and down his pecs, ruffling the light hair in the process. He felt so warm, so solid, and wrapped up in his arms was her new favourite place.

The sex hadn't been bad, either.

Thea smiled. Now, that was an understatement of epic proportions. He'd been—they'd been, together—utterly fantastic, and her body was still thanking him for the many intense orgasms he'd given her. She felt dreamy, relaxed, yet not willing to waste a moment with him by sleeping.

Thea heard the faint smack of a wave hitting the rocks below and cocked her head. 'The tide is coming in,' she murmured.

Farrell stroked her hair. 'Mm, it must be about four o'clock in the morning,' he told her.

She groaned, turned her head and pushed her nose into his chest. They'd spent a good portion of yesterday making love and all of the night. Frankly, she couldn't think of a better way to have passed those hours.

'Ugh, I've got an interview with your resort manager at eight,' she muttered. She'd far prefer to sleep in, but she'd made the appointment the day she got here, and she couldn't change it now. Besides, she'd done minimal work while on the island, and she needed to make a lot of notes today, gather her impressions and start outlining her article. She knew she was going to highlight the work Farrell was doing to make this island ecologically sustainable, and the ethos of working with nature, not against it. She'd fallen in love with Petit Saphir, and somehow felt emotionally connected to the island...

But was that because of the location, or because of Farrell? Could she separate the two? She knew this island was exceedingly important to him, and was that knowledge rubbing off on her? More worrying, was she, because she was attracted to him and had slept with him, developing feelings for him? He'd been charismatic and hot back then, hadn't been a guy she could easily ignore, but he'd changed, not beyond recognition, but substantially.

She was so into the man he'd become…quietly funny, intensely smart, so aware. Had something caused this change in him, or had he simply grown up? Curiosity crawled under her skin.

Thea felt Farrell pull back, and she lifted her head to see him looking down at her. 'What?' she asked, smiling at his ruffled hair and the satisfaction in his eyes.

'I thought you might've fallen asleep,' he said.

'No, I was just thinking.'

'About?'

She hesitated, not wanting to open old wounds or destroy their relaxed intimacy. So she changed the subject. 'Some of your guests flew out this morning; it's day five and I can move into my own villa.'

'You're not going anywhere,' Farrell immediately responded.

All righty, then. And, let's be honest, after the past eighteen hours, it would take a nuclear strike to dislodge her.

'Now tell me what you were really thinking about,' he demanded.

Thea wrinkled her nose. Busted.

Should she mention the past? Go there? It

hadn't been a fun time for either of them, but there was no point in ignoring the elephant in the room. 'I was thinking about you, back then.'

He grimaced. 'You were wondering how you ended up sleeping with the biggest jerk on campus?' He sounded bitter, and Thea didn't want that. Not after everything they'd just shared.

She sat up, pulling the sheet up and tucking it under her arms. She looked out of the window, biting her lip. He'd been annoying, but she didn't want to hurt his feelings by confirming it. Besides, it was all in the past...

He moved up the bed to lean against the headboard and rested his arm on her bended knee. 'I'm very aware that I was self-involved and arrogant, Thea. You don't need to sugar-coat it for me. I had far too much money and believed that my last name made me better than everyone else.'

Thea grimaced at his harsh tone. 'That was twelve years ago, Farrell,' she said, stroking his arm. 'You're not that guy any more.'

He looked at her. 'How do you know?' he demanded. 'How do you know I'm not?'

She heard a hint of desperation, a need to be believed in his voice, the hope. 'You talk nicely to your staff, you're polite. The boy you were would never spend time on a dive boat rehabilitating a reef, he'd think it was beneath him.

I also heard that you took Gwen and another journalist to the mainland. The person you were would've delegated that task to someone else. You care deeply about this island, and you care about your staff. Farrell-back-then only cared about himself.'

Farrell surprised her by leaning forward, placing his lips on her forehead and kissing her for a heartbeat or two. Forehead kisses were entirely underrated, Thea decided. Especially when you got one from a masculine, rugged man. Farrell pulled back and sent her a soft smile. 'Thank you for saying that.' He rubbed his hand down his face. 'Did I properly apologise for being so mean to you at uni?'

'You did. And we agreed to let it go.'

Farrell nodded and leaned back, pulling up his legs. He looked past her and Thea looked over her shoulder to see the first hint of the incoming sunrise. She really should get some sleep, or she'd be less than useless later.

'Can I ask you a question?'

She swallowed her yawn and nodded. He opened his arm, and she scooted closer to him, curling up into him, her head back on his chest. She was so tired, so relaxed and…yes, happy. It felt strange and nice. She yawned again and felt her eyes closing.

'Why were you so prickly back then? I mean,

I understand your attitude towards me, and I deserved it, but why did you keep everyone else at a distance too?'

She was so tired, but she forced the words out. 'Because there's nothing worse than people being nice to you, then turning around and disappointing you. It's always better to keep your distance, to stay apart. That way I don't get hurt.'

Thea winced at her honesty, but she was too sleepy to police her words. In the morning, she'd shore up her defences, rebuild the walls that had developed cracks while she was making love with Farrell. When she woke up, she'd remind herself that this was just sex, that nothing was bubbling between them, that they were just two consenting adults who found each other attractive. Nothing more, nothing less, and definitely nothing deeper.

Thea wrapped her arm around his waist and rubbed her cheek on his pec, loving his masculine skin, the tang of his soap hitting her nose. Her eyes felt as heavy as cinderblocks, and her body sank into him. She'd sleep for a couple of hours, and later she'd gather herself up and regroup.

But for a few hours, she'd use this marvellous man as her pillow.

Later that day, Thea tumbled off her paddleboard and hit the soup-warm water. Farrell watched as she allowed herself to sink, easily catching her frustrated expression through the super clear water. She had terrible hand-eye coordination and even worse balance.

Thea pushed herself off the sandy bottom and broke the surface of the water, raking her hair back off her face. Her face was shiny from waterproof sunblock, and her eyes sparkled in the sunlight.

She slapped her hand against the side of the rocking paddleboard. 'Stupid thing,' she muttered.

'Don't blame the equipment because you suck,' Farrell cheerfully told her. He shook his head, amused. 'I have never met anyone with worse balance than you.'

She glared at him, highly unimpressed. 'That's not something the owner of a resort should say to a journalist,' she told him, lifting her nose in the air. 'I might be tempted to give you a bad review.'

He looked down at her, grinning. 'We agreed that when we were alone, then we were just you and me, with no titles or occupations.' They'd had a brief conversation about boundaries this morning after a round of superfast, super hot sex in the shower. It had taken place in between brushing their teeth, rinsing and flossing. Not ideal, but Thea had been in a rush to make her appointment with his general manager. But yes, they'd agreed to keep their work and personal lives separate.

That being said, he couldn't help wondering if he was making a mistake. Every time he looked at Thea, felt her hand brush his, or heard her laugh, part of him wanted to throw caution to the wind and throw himself into loving her. But another part—heavier, sharper—reminded him of who he was and the secrets he carried. Beneath the charm, the polish, the carefully measured smiles, he was still a man who had spent his life hiding behind surfaces, pretending. He had a reputation for being calm, unflappable, charismatic, but nobody had ever seen the real him, and he wasn't sure anyone ever could.

Yet here Thea was, silently daring him to show her. He loved her mind, the way she saw things clearly, the curve of her smile, the spark in her eyes, the warmth of her personality wrapping around him. He wanted to give her more of him—but the past clung to him, his uninvited companion. The company, the misdeeds buried beneath its success, the guilt he'd inherited via his father's actions—they were his burden. Anyone discovering the truth would be a disaster. Thea finding out? That would be a nightmare of epic proportions. Because what if she found him wanting? Or worse, indelibly tainted?

He watched her now, perched on the board at his feet, legs dangling in the water, wet hair plastered against her back. Underneath the desire and the heat was fear—hard and acidic. Yet he still wanted her. Wanted the danger, the thrill, the closeness that made the world outside his villa vanish. He wanted to fold her into his arms and hold her there for ever, even knowing that doing so meant exposing the parts of himself he usually kept buried. For the first time in a long while, he realised some risks—some people—were worth everything, even if the fall was terrifying.

And, God, she was such an enormous risk. His biggest temptation. Hurt waiting to happen—

Thea looked around the empty bay. 'I know that some of the journalists and all of your investors have left, but, remind me, where did the rest of your guests go?' she asked. She'd been rushing and hadn't checked the itinerary. She didn't need to: Farrell had all the information she needed whenever she needed it.

Farrell widened his feet, the paddleboard rocking below them. 'They went snorkelling,' he told her, 'on a reef off an island a few hours from here.'

She wrinkled her nose. 'Why didn't I go, again?' she asked him, her smile flirtatious. He grinned, dropped to his haunches and then, without warning, tumbled her off the board into the water. Thea came up from her dunking, laughing. He trod water as he kissed her lips. Good grief, she was intoxicating, and he couldn't get enough of her.

He returned to her question. 'You're not with them because I suggested another way to spend the day,' he said, banding his arm around her small waist. 'I wanted to stay in bed all day, but you hauled me out here and insisted I teach you how to paddleboard.'

She hooked her arm around his neck, smiling. 'You're a terrible teacher,' she told him. 'I keep falling off.'

'That's because you have the balance of a puppy on crack,' Farrell retorted, kissing her nose. He gripped her board, which was threatening to float away, and her with his other arm. He looked up at the sky, then glanced at his waterproof sports watch. 'It's mid-afternoon, and we haven't had lunch yet.'

'Mm, I suggested it, but, once again, we got distracted.'

Frankly, if there was a choice between Thea and food, he'd starve. Any day of the week and twice on Sundays. 'Shall I order up a picnic basket from the kitchen?'

She nodded enthusiastically, looking at the loungers under the palm trees. 'Can you order a couple of beers, too? There's nothing better than a cold beer after being in the sea on a hot day.'

She was definitely a girl after his own heart. 'Sounds good. But instead of eating it on the beach, why don't we jump on a jet ski and go somewhere else?'

Thea hung onto the paddleboard as he kicked their way to the beach. 'Where?' she asked.

'Somewhere private,' Farrell told her. Somewhere he could strip her down and make love to her on a towel on the beach. Or up against a boulder. In the sea.

Thea poked him in the chest. 'That sounds good, but, seriously, food first.'

He nodded. But he couldn't guarantee it, not when she was tastier than anything he'd experienced. Ever.

CHAPTER EIGHT

ON A SMALL, uninhabited island north of Petit Saphir, Thea, a bottle of beer in her hand, squinted at the dying sun—swathes of pink and purple and orange painted across the sky—and popped a grape into her mouth. She sat on a towel on the still-warm sand, her wet hair hanging down her back. Her back was to Farrell's chest, his long legs on either side of hers. He rested his chin on her head and his hand on her stomach. 'Shouldn't we think about heading back?' she asked. 'It's getting dark.'

'Mm,' Farrell murmured. 'I know the route back, there's a headlight on the jet ski, and the moon is still pretty full. I spent many nights on this island when I was a teenager.'

'By yourself?' she asked.

'Sometimes, yes. When I was older, I'd bring friends here and we'd camp here for days.'

Thea rested the back of her head on his collarbone as Farrell snagged a grape from the bunch in her hand. 'Your childhood sounds idyllic,' she stated.

'It might sound like it, but that doesn't mean it was,' Farrell cryptically replied.

Thea waited, but after a minute—maybe more—she realised he had no intention of elaborating. While he could often talk about any subject under the sun, he rarely, okay, never, made personal observations or gave her any indication about how he was feeling.

Farrell Wolfe wasn't a closed book; he was a super-secure, couldn't-be-hacked vault. Although, while he never gave anything personal away himself, he seemed super interested in her. In her past, in how she was feeling, anything she could tell him. Having his attention on her was…dizzying. She'd never stood in the spotlight of someone's attention before, and she was thoroughly enjoying it.

'Where did you go when you needed some space?'

She frowned at his left-field question. 'Sorry? What?'

'When you wanted space from your parents, where did you go?'

She pulled her knees up and leaned forward, wrapping her arms around her knees. While Farrell had escaped to empty Indian Ocean islands to get some space from his family, she'd spent her time trying to stay off her parents' radar. And when she'd left, she'd done it in the most drastic way possible.

'My family wasn't like yours, Farrell.'

He moved so that he sat to the side of her, able to see her face. She darted a look at him and saw the mixture of concern and worry on his face. 'I remember a rumour from uni…something about you being totally self-supporting, that you worked three jobs to pay your rent, your tuition fees and your living expenses.'

Sometimes the grapevine relayed the right gossip. 'Yes, that's true.'

'Why didn't your parents help you out?'

There it was—the question she'd been waiting for. Now she had to decide whether to answer him or not, or to change the subject as he did when she asked a too-personal question. They could carry on sleeping together, being surface-level buddies who enjoyed each other in bed, or they could drop into deeper territory. Did she want Farrell to know about her past, to understand why she'd been tense and prickly, snarky and snappy? Did she want him to know why that time of her life had been so damn hard? She thought she did.

'My parents didn't help me fund my education because I didn't ask them to,' she quietly told him. 'They didn't know I was attending uni, what I was studying. By that point, we hadn't spoken for a few years.'

She could see the questions in his eyes…had she been a drug addict? A chronic runaway? A wild child who couldn't be controlled? Thea sighed. People always assumed the parents were right and the kid was the problem. But she'd tried, she really had…

Farrell moved closer to her, slid his leg under her bent knees, and placed a hand on her back. 'Can you tell me, Thea?'

'I was estranged from my parents,' she murmured. 'Basically, I was on my own from sixteen.'

She looked at him, saw the shock on his face, the horror stories scrambling through his brain. She shook her head, eager to reassure him. 'I didn't live on the streets, I wasn't a runaway, I didn't do drugs, and I wasn't kicked out. It was my choice to leave home.'

Relief and confusion replaced his horror. 'But…why?'

She'd said too much, much more than she'd meant to. This was the first real, personal conversation she'd had since she'd stopped therapy, her defences lowered by Farrell's steady warmth, his attentiveness, the way he made her feel as though what she said mattered. But Thea knew better. People felt one way today, another tomorrow. Within the blink of an eye, he could grow bored, irritated, and distant, and she'd learned not to expect consistency.

Once, when she was younger, she'd craved connection and a sense of belonging. But experience had taught her that the moment she leaned in, when she began to trust, there was an excellent chance it would be yanked away, leaving her adrift. She wanted to believe in people. God, she wanted to believe in Farrell. But she'd long ago learned to see life as it was, not as she wished it to be. Detachment was safer. Distance was survival. If her parents hadn't given her the emotional stability every child needed, how could she expect anyone, especially a holiday fling, to hold steady?

She drained her beer and pushed the grape stalk into the neck of the bottle. Standing up, she dusted sand off her thighs and her bottom and gestured to the falling night. 'I really think we should head back,' she said briskly, wrapping a sarong around her hips.

Farrell climbed to his feet and tipped his head to the side. 'Do you really want to go, or do you just want to stop talking about your past?'

Look at him, so observant and perceptive. Thea shrugged as she pulled on her T-shirt. 'Both?'

Farrell pushed her hair back behind her ear

and stepped forward to kiss her temple. 'Fair enough,' he murmured. 'Let's go back.'

She appreciated his easy acceptance, the way he didn't demand more than she could give. But a small part of her was disappointed too. Because she wanted to tell him. She just…needed a nudge. A question, a coax, a quick tug to tip her over the edge. Sure, silence was easier, distance was safer—but…damn.

She also wanted him to open up to her, to give her more of an insight into what he was thinking and feeling. She didn't want to be the only one standing on the edge of an emotional cliff, contemplating the rocks below. She wanted him to take the plunge too.

Thea watched as Farrell folded up the towel and bent down to place their empty bottles in the backpacks they were using instead of a picnic basket. She swung hers onto her shoulders, surprised at how much lighter it felt. So, she realised, did her heart. She hadn't told Farrell much—she'd barely scratched the surface—but somehow the reality of her childhood didn't feel as heavy. That was new. And a little dangerous.

The next day, instead of joining the small group of journalists left on the island for full-body massage treatments on the beach, Thea decided to explore the rest of the island on foot. Five days might be enough time for some journalists to get a feel for the island, but she needed as much time as possible to dig beneath its pretty packaging. With a water bottle in her backpack, a bikini under her lightweight, long-sleeved cotton button-down and khaki shorts, sturdy sandals on her feet, she walked up the resort's main beach, skirted bits of what could be called a mini-jungle and emerged into an area that was strictly 'behind-the-scenes'.

Thea looked around and took in what looked to be a workshop, a storage room and the laundry room. Sheets flapped on a long washing line, and the open doors of what looked to be a smaller stockroom revealed dive equipment, buoyancy vests, fins and masks, all neatly stored. Thea saw a steel jetty in the distance and watched staff members, all dressed in the resort's aqua T-shirts and black shorts, climbing into a large rigid inflatable boat. She glanced at her watch and saw that it was the change of shift. These people were heading home…

Curious, she walked towards the jetty, her heart fluttering when she saw Farrell at the tiller, dark sunglasses over his eyes. As if he sensed her, his head turned, and he slowly pushed his shades up into his hair and beckoned her to walk down the jetty.

'You lost?' he asked when she approached the

boat. She shook her head. 'Aren't you supposed to be enjoying a full-body massage right now?'

While she liked the idea of a full-body massage, she wasn't a fan of sharing the experience with other people. No, she'd experience the world-class spa facilities on her own later. She shrugged. 'I wanted to do something different,' she said. She watched as his staff members settled onto the bench seat, wondering where they were going and why Farrell was driving the boat. He was the CEO—didn't he have better things to do with his time?

He smiled up at her. 'Do you want to come for a ride?' he asked, nodding to the spare seat on the other side of the tiller. 'I'm doing the staff run and need to have a quick chat with the head of the village on Grande Saphir.'

She couldn't think of a better way to spend her time, so Thea instantly agreed. She stepped into the boat and over feet to reach her seat. As Farrell started the boat, she pulled her hair back into a tight ponytail to keep it from whipping her face. The engine caught, and Farrell checked that they weren't missing any people. He reversed the boat, hit the throttle, and the next minute they were skimming across the flat sea. Thea held her hand up to her eyes, wishing she'd remembered her sunglasses because the glare off the water was intense. She felt a nudge on her shoulder and turned. Farrell held out his sunglasses.

She shook her head. 'I'm sure you need them more than me,' she told him.

'I'm fine,' he told her. 'Use them.'

Thea slipped them onto her face—they were too big and warm from the sun—but she immediately felt the difference, now able to take in the hues of the ocean, the hints of a small reef, an island in the distance.

'We employ all of our staff from a neighbouring island,' Farrell told her, his voice carrying above the wind. 'The staff are ferried to and from work, and it takes about ten minutes.'

Thea nodded, happy to divide her attention between the way the wind plastered Farrell's shirt to his chest, and ruffled his hair, his easy confidence as he handled the fast, powerful boat, and the green island coming into view. It was the same one she'd seen from the air when she'd first arrived. A couple of boats, a little beaten and battered, bobbed next to the jetty, and men sat on cool-drink crates in the hot sun, mending fishing nets. They all looked up as the boat puttered up to the jetty, and the skinniest of the three men stood up and caught the rope and tied it to a steel cleat.

With the nimbleness and confidence of people who'd done this a thousand times, Farrell's employees stepped from the inflatable onto the jetty and exchanged bright smiles and greetings with the elderly men on the deck. When they were all off the boat, Farrell picked up his backpack and a cardboard box and looked at her.

'Hold on a sec, and I'll help you,' he told her. Before she could respond, he stepped off the boat and placed the box on the deck, holding out a hand. She slid hers into his and stepped onto the boat's rim and then the jetty. She thanked him, greeted the elders, and watched as Farrell bent down and picked up the box again.

'What's in there?' she asked as she walked next to him.

'Some supplies for the clinic,' he said, sounding surprised that she'd asked. 'Antibiotics, pain killers, gauze and such. Contraceptives.'

She waited as Farrell greeted some ladies sitting at a plastic table outside what looked to be a basic general store. 'There's a clinic on this island?' she asked, impressed. His sunglasses slid down her nose, and she impatiently pushed them up.

'And a primary school,' he told her. 'The older kids have the option of staying on the island and completing high school via virtual classrooms.'

Thea's eyebrows rose. She'd visited many developing countries over the past few years, and when she'd ventured out of the swish tourist spots, she'd found a lot of poverty and few services. But the streets on this island were clean, the houses newly painted, and every building sported solar panels.

Impressive. Seriously.

'Most of our staff on Petit Saphir come from this island,' Farrell told her, as a young man exited a bright yellow house, a doctor's coat over his T-shirt and board shorts. His eyes dropped to the box Farrell held, and he bounded over to him.

'You brought it!' he said, obviously excited. 'Thanks, Farrell.'

Farrell transferred the box to the man's open arms, and Thea caught his grunt as the heavy box sank in his grip. Farrell had carried it as if it weighed nothing at all. 'Thea, meet Dr Saul Lablanche. He visits the island once a week and works as a doctor on Mahé. He's on standby if we have any disasters on Grande and Petit Saphir.'

Thea greeted Dr Saul, and he shot her a smile as he opened the box with one hand. 'Did you manage to get the anaesthesia drugs I asked for?' he asked Farrell.

'Kyle said to tell you everything is there and to stop bugging him,' Farrell replied, his tone amused. 'And he'd far prefer it, for legal reasons, if you'd wait until you got to the mainland before removing an appendix.'

Thea winced, but Saul simply shrugged. 'I didn't have time, and my patient would've died if we'd waited for air transport. It was safer to whip it out.'

He sounded so blasé, and Thea imagined him wielding a scalpel in his consulting room. 'Um… is the patient okay?' she asked.

Farrell put his hand on her back, smiling. 'No need to worry, Thea. Saul is a licensed general surgeon, and his wife, and travelling companion, is not only a licensed doctor but a qualified anaesthetist, too. There's a small, but perfectly functional, theatre within the clinic.'

Thea placed a hand on her heart, relieved and impressed. How did this tiny island manage to be this well resourced? She pondered the question as she walked next to Farrell to a small, official-looking building. Farrell ushered her up the stairs to the deep, cool veranda.

'This is the courthouse, community centre and where I meet the village head,' he explained. He gestured to the wooden bench that sat up against the wall and told her to take a seat. 'I should be about a half-hour, if that's okay. I'll send someone out with something to drink. It's cooler to wait out here than inside.'

A cold drink sounded wonderful. 'That's fine,' she told him, happy to watch the busy street as the villagers went about their daily business.

Farrell nodded, and he slipped into the building, the door snicking closed behind him. She pushed his sunglasses up into her hair and removed her backpack, dropping it into the space between her feet. Leaning her back against the cool wall, she smiled as a pair of young women left the building, the smaller of the two very pregnant. They spoke in a mixture of English and Creole, their conversation melodious. A man on a bicycle sped past on the road below, adroitly ducking pedestrians, waving his hand at a fruit seller who shouted something at him as he rode past.

She loved seeing this slice of island life; it was so very different from the resort lifestyle. It was real, with a cast of characters who lived their lives here.

A soft clearing of a throat pulled her attention to her right, and she saw a stunning Seychelloise woman standing a yard away, holding a glass full of ice and a can of soda. Thea hoped that was for her.

'Thea?'

'Hi!' Thea nodded to the glass. 'Is that for me?'

'Farrell asked me to bring it to you.'

'Thank you so much.'

'Farrell asked me to answer any questions you might have about Grande Saphir.'

Oh, yay! Thea patted the bench next to her, happy to talk to someone her own age. Having someone, a local, to answer her questions was a godsend, and Thea, between gulps of soda, peppered Marie with questions about her life, her past and the island. After twenty minutes, she had the bare bones of Marie's story—she was the eldest daughter of the village head, educated on the mainland, and was now an occupational therapist, home on leave. Thea listened, mentally cataloguing details of the island and its people, wishing she had her camera and notebook but settling instead for committing every word to memory. What struck her most was how different the island was from what she'd expected, and that the glossy improvements were recent, the result, not of government aid, but conceived and paid for by Farrell.

Marie described how Farrell, five years ago, had returned day after day until her father had agreed to listen to his vision of developing the two islands. Instead of immediately demanding permission to build his resort, Farrell had pledged to upgrade houses, build a school and a clinic, install solar, provide running water, and relocate the handful of families living on Petit Saphir into better homes—all before breaking ground or getting a signed, legal agreement stating he could build his resort.

Against all expectations, he had delivered on his promises, pouring millions into the island, employing dozens, sponsoring education, and transforming daily life. Thea sat stunned, grappling with the absurdity of a developer investing so much without any guarantees, unable to reconcile the reckless arrogance of the boy she remembered with the man who had given so much to this island.

She couldn't believe he'd take such a big risk on something that might not pan out. That he'd spent millions without a backup plan in place. 'It's absurd,' she muttered, then waved her words away. 'I mean, I'm so glad the island got developed, but that he did it without any agreement in place is a bit mind-blowing.'

'My father calls him his favourite madman,' Marie said, smiling. She looked at her watch, stood up and held out her hand for Thea to shake. 'It was nice meeting you, Thea.'

'You too,' Thea replied. 'Thanks for talking to me.'

Marie turned to walk back into the building as Farrell stepped out. They exchanged a quick hug and had a quick discussion about her dad, who seemed to be suffering from a chest infection. Farrell kissed her cheek goodbye and walked over to Thea, his hands in his pockets of his chino shorts. 'Hey, did I take too long?' he asked.

'No, I was chatting to Marie,' she said, picking up her backpack and standing up.

Farrell took her backpack from her and slipped it over his shoulder. He tipped his head to the side. 'You have a weird look on your face. Is everything okay?'

She wanted to digest what she'd heard, try to make sense of it, before she asked him about it. 'I'm fine,' she said.

Instead of pushing for more, he led her down the stairs and back onto the street. 'Are you in a hurry to get back to the resort?' he asked.

She shook her head. 'No. Why?'

'Do you want to see something pretty cool?' he asked.

Thea smiled at him. 'I'm a travel writer, Wolfe. I always want to see something cool.'

The forest on the far side of Grande Saphir was a lush tangle of green and smelled of damp earth and salt carried in from the sea. Giant palms arched overhead, their fronds jiggling in the slight breeze, and Farrell pointed out cinnamon and takamaka trees. Sunlight pierced the canopy in scattered beams, bright birds flitted through the branches above, and lizards skittered across the path. The whole place felt alive, humming as nature went about its business.

Then the trees ended, and there it was—tucked away, impossibly lovely. It was a swimming hole, carved from black volcanic rock, with water a shade of blue Thea had never encountered before. Above the pool, a thin waterfall spilt over a ledge and hit the water, reminding Thea of a wedding veil. Thea stood on a flat boulder next to the pool, looked down and saw tiny fish flashing through the water. This was a place to get lost in, to linger, to remember—

'It's lovely, isn't it?'

Farrell's voice broke through, and she turned to face him, her hand on her heart. 'It's stunning...utterly breathtaking.'

He pulled his phone from his pocket and placed it, and the keys to the off-road dirt bike he'd borrowed, onto a flat-topped rock. He grabbed his collar behind his neck and pulled off his shirt in that movement that men seemed to master at birth. She'd slept with him many times now, but the sight of his body could still rip the breath from her lungs.

She swallowed at the expanse of his muscled chest, his flat, ridged stomach, a light layer of hair disappearing into his shorts. His eyes caught hers, and she wondered why he looked so serious. 'You can't write about this place, Thea. Actually, everything, from the time you got onto the boat this morning, until you get back to the resort, is off the record.'

Thea was caught off guard by him pushing his shorts down his long, muscled thighs. Was he intending to strip off completely? The moisture in her mouth dried up as Farrell stood in a pair of tight black boxer briefs that left very little to the imagination. Lord, the man had a very nice package. And he knew how to use it.

She shook her head, trying to get her brain to restart. What did he say? 'Why off the record?' she asked, bemused.

He sent her a look with those dark, mysterious eyes, the exact colour of the encroaching jungle bordering this thoroughly magical swimming hole. 'If you describe it in your usual evocative, compelling way, it won't be hard for tourists to find this island, and this spot. The islanders don't mind the odd tourist, but they don't want to be hassled by boatloads of them.'

It was hard to think when he stood in front of her, nearly naked, looking so utterly gorgeous. 'But wouldn't tourists be good for the island? Wouldn't they bring in a lot of revenue?'

His eyebrows rose. 'In case you didn't notice, the island is thriving without tourists.'

She wrinkled her nose, then nodded. 'You

support the island,' she stated, her brain kicking in.

'There's a trust, and when the resort starts earning, they will also get a percentage of the profits from the resort.' Farrell looked into the pool. 'They don't need to chase tourist dollars.'

Thea bit her lip. Between visiting this watering hole, and the island, and her conversation with Marie, she was passing up an amazing opportunity to provide more depth to her article, to her writing, to let the world know more about Farrell Wolfe, to allow the world to see below the surface of the inscrutable travel entrepreneur and his amazing resort.

But when he'd invited her to join him today, he'd invited her, Thea Monroe, and not the writer of *Thea Travels*. And if he asked her to keep this off the record, then she had no choice but to respect his wishes.

But she could push a little. 'Are you sure?' she asked. 'It would be great copy.'

He smiled and shook his head. 'Let's just pretend you aren't a journalist and I'm not Wolfe International's CEO, okay?'

She could push further, but she knew it wouldn't help. Farrell wasn't a man she could budge. Thea looked at the deep pool and started to open the buttons on her shirt, grateful she'd pulled on a bikini earlier in the day. 'Is it deep enough to dive?'

He flashed her a smile, seemingly grateful that she'd changed the subject. 'It's a small pool, so I'd far prefer it if you did a straight-leg jump.' She looked at the drop, and estimated it to be about twelve feet.

'You up for it?' he asked, lifting a challenging eyebrow.

Thea nodded. 'This isn't the scariest thing I've done,' she said. Nothing came close to the fear she'd experienced when she'd ventured out into the world on her own at sixteen. She shook off the memories of her parents' casual acceptance of her leaving, pushed back the hurt, and tossed Farrell a big smile. 'I recently went white water rafting in Oregon, rappelled in the Alps, and took a trip in a hot-air balloon in Cappadocia, so it's not even the scariest thing I've done in the last six months.'

And with that, Thea stepped out of her shorts, walked over to the edge of the short cliff, but was stopped by Farrell's hand on her arm. He shook his head, and Thea frowned. 'Problem?'

'Mm,' he said, his hand snaking around her back to pull at the ties holding her bikini top together. 'Local lore says that you have to be naked the first time you swim here or else you'll have bad luck for a year.'

She lifted her eyebrows. 'Is that the lore according to Farrell?'

Farrell tugged her bikini top over her head and let it fall, his mouth brushing hers as his thumbs hooked into the sides of her bottoms and slid them down her hips. 'Swim naked with me, Thea. Let's make a memory.'

He stripped, hauled her against him, and then they were airborne—plunging feet first into the pool. The shock of the cold water punched the air from her lungs, and she came up gasping, pushing wet hair from her eyes. He came up right next to her, his grin suggesting this was the best idea in the world, and his mouth covered hers. Her legs wound around his hips instinctively, body answering his without hesitation.

The water was cool, but her skin burned. Every nerve ending sparked, and her breath hitched when she realised that the walls she'd oh-so-carefully built were in danger of crumbling. And when Farrell pulled back to look at her and lifted a strand of wet hair off her cheek, she caught the tenderness in his gaze. She swallowed. This was more than just a kiss in a hidden pool on a hot summer's day, more than a holiday fling.

He was, she reluctantly admitted, going to be very difficult to walk away from.

CHAPTER NINE

Farrell, not finding Kyle in the office they shared at the resort, walked onto the wooden balcony and found him standing in the corner, smoking a cigarette and scowling at the mirror-flat ocean. The guests, including Thea, were snorkelling over a pristine reef north of the Petit Saphir. He'd wanted to join them, but he had a pile of work to get through. Instead of spending hours at his desk at night, as he normally did, he'd been stopping work early to spend time with Thea and was days behind. When she'd asked him to join them, he'd reminded her—and himself—he had other resorts to run, business decisions to make, reports to read. When he missed details and didn't pay attention, things went wrong.

He watched Kyle take a long drag, and his stomach dropped; Kyle only ever smoked when he was stressed. 'What's up?' he asked, coming to stand beside him. He pulled his sunglasses from his shirt pocket and slid them over his eyes.

It was a stunning summer's day, and it was a sacrilege to spend it inside. He'd made progress this morning; maybe he could take the inflatable and join Thea and the rest of the guests on the reef.

Damn it, no. He was going to stand here for five minutes, and then he was going back to his spreadsheets and income and expense reports, staff evaluations and cash-flow statements.

'We have a problem,' Kyle said, blowing smoke out of his nose.

'I gathered that,' Farrell replied. 'What is it?'

'The publicity department received an email asking you to comment on the destruction of a reef and mangrove forest during the construction of the Vunilagi Sands resort in Fiji. That was one your dad developed, right?'

Farrell gripped the bridge of his nose between his index finger and his thumb. He closed his eyes and cursed. His heart rate increased. 'Why are they asking me to comment on old news? My father developed it over twenty years ago, and we don't own it any more.'

'You know that doesn't matter,' Kyle responded. 'The email mentions blatant corruption by WI employees, bribes, wilful destruction of the environment and a corporate attitude of profits first.'

Shit. 'Does the journalist have proof?'

Kyle shrugged. 'He simply asked for a response.' Then he frowned. 'Wasn't one of your first donations from the foundation to a community and mangrove restoration project in Fiji? Is this related?'

Damn, he was sharp. 'My father authorised every bribe and bulldozer. He was fully aware of the damage he was causing to the reef and the forest. He didn't care; he wanted a spa on stilts, and the environment wasn't being cooperative, so he removed it.'

Kyle winced and cursed.

Farrell gripped the railing, his knuckles turning white. 'How did this come to light and why now?'

'Apparently the journalist writing the piece is Fijian and an environmental activist.' Yeah, that would do it. There had been a massive outcry at the time, but his father had managed to squash it, to put out the PR fires using corporate clout and a lot of money.

'People were involved, Farrell, and people can't keep their mouths shut for ever,' Kyle said. 'If the story is that one of WI's flagship resorts only went ahead because your father bribed local politicians to override environmental protections, it's going to cause a media storm.'

Farrell didn't bother to tell Kyle his father had also paid off scientists to produce a fake impact study. He stared at the horizon, his gut roiling like a cyclonic tide. How much did the journalist actually know? What evidence did he have? Did he have solid proof that his father had known, signed off on and greased the wheels that had let bulldozers tear through coral and mangrove forests? Did he know about the other resorts? A sour, metallic taste filled Farrell's mouth. Was the journalist simply fishing, casting bait in the hope he would bite? How far had the story spread? Was he just starting his investigation, or was the story already written? And, if published, how would it be received, and what impact would it have on Wolfe International?

'The timing is interesting,' Farrell stated, panic licking his throat, 'especially as we are hosting journalists who are writing about my latest, fully sustainable resort.'

'I had the same thought,' Kyle said. 'Do you think there's a connection to anyone here?'

Farrell thought about it for a minute. 'Not unless they have someone working in Fiji,' he said. He'd buried all the WI documentation in a fully encrypted, off-site data warehouse. 'If there is information to be found, it would be from there, from local people who were impacted, from government officials who were paid off.'

Kyle sighed and placed his forearms on the railing. 'If this story breaks at the same time the promo articles about this place land, the contrast will go viral. That's not what we want.'

He'd had the same thought.

'You can get ahead of it, Farrell, if you respond immediately,' Kyle quietly suggested. 'It was before your time; you were only a teenager. The times were different; you weren't in charge. You have a solid history and commitment, and a proven track record in creating sustainable projects. If you do that, WI will withstand the PR hit.'

He disagreed because he knew he'd instantly be accused of greenwashing, of saying one thing and doing another. Every mistake he'd made would be raked up, his every decision questioned. His, and WI's, record on eco-sustainability would be analysed and they'd be found lacking. Kyle didn't understand, because Farrell had never told anyone how his father's actions had affected him personally. How he'd been forced to look into a mirror and confront the man he was…vain, spoiled, entitled. How he'd had to rewrite his values, how he'd examined his entire life, taken it apart and put it back together again. How he worried that he'd slip back into being the person he was before, how tough he was on himself. How, at his core, he was ashamed to be his father's son.

Would he spend the rest of his life paying for

his father's mistakes, his greed? How much did he have to give of himself to make amends and to rebalance the scales? How many millions did he have to donate, how many trees did he have to plant, reefs to rehabilitate, to make a dent in the debt his family owed the environment?

Would it ever end?

He looked out to sea, his thoughts returning to Thea. She wrote about ecologically sustainable resorts, promoted the companies committed to looking after the environment. What would she think of Wolfe International, of him, if, or when, the news about Vunilagi broke? Because it would break. If the reporter had got as far as asking for environmental sustainability impact studies, he, or she, already had their suspicions. And they'd find the proof. The right questions, the right money and persistence would blow the story wide open.

Would Thea see this as a betrayal by, not just his father, but, by extension, him? It wasn't his signature on those papers, but he knew the sins of the father were inherited by the son. Would she be prepared to listen to his side of the story, or would she judge him on what she read online and in the newspapers? More to the point, would he be able to tell her his side of the story, how he'd changed, his guilt…the mess he was beneath his polished shell?

Explaining would mean getting very personal, exposing the soft skin of his emotional underbelly. They'd only been sleeping together for a short time; she'd only been on the island for a week, they were just having a fling, some hot island sex.

It felt like a lot longer than a week, and like so much more than a fling. Images of them back home in London, or New York, often floated through his brain. Breakfast together in his Canal Walk flat, weekends away at his cottage in Oxfordshire. Weekend trips to Vienna or Prague, walking hand in hand through parks and galleries, laughing over expensive meals and street food… But being in a relationship meant getting real and—God—he didn't think he could do it.

'Ignore the email—it's too vague and the journalist could be fishing. If he goes into details, let me know,' Farrell stated, his head throbbing with the beginnings of a headache.

There was nothing he could do but watch and wait. But somehow, he knew, deep down, it wouldn't be long before the sky fell.

'Are you okay?'

Thea sat on the edge of her lounger, her feet digging into the hot sand. It was mid-afternoon, and the rest of Farrell's guests were in their villas, lying under the air conditioner and napping after a deliciously decadent lunch following their trip to the reef. Knowing she had to work off the many calories she'd eaten, she'd slipped into Farrell's office and invited him down to the beach for a swim, and had been surprised when he'd agreed.

They'd swum out to the buoy and back, with Farrell's strong strokes pulling him far ahead. Why had his fast pace given her the impression he'd been trying to outswim a demon or two? She stared at his profile, took in the hint of a frown. He was, at best, preoccupied. At worst, worried.

He didn't answer her. 'Farrell?' she prompted him.

He finally looked at her. 'Mm?'

'What's going on? You're a million miles away.'

'Nothing, I'm fine.' Yeah, that was a big, fat whopper. But she wasn't surprised by him not explaining. He rarely told her anything personal, and when their conversation wandered into his family or childhood, even his time at university, he adroitly changed the subject, either with humour or by asking her a question, and the moment passed.

He was exceptionally good at not giving anything away. Thea gnawed the inside of her cheek. Did he not trust her? Was he worried that she'd use anything he said for her article? 'You can talk to me, you know. I'd never reveal anything you say as my lover.'

He ran his hand through his wet hair and gestured to the bay, glistening under the summer sun. 'It might be paradise, but I'm still working, Thea. I can't be in holiday mode all the time.'

Thea heard the snap in his tone and, just like that, a wall sprang up between them. She suddenly realised that not once during the last forty-five minutes had Farrell touched her. He was, normally, quite affectionate, often placing his hand on her back, on her knee, or threading his hand through hers.

In contrast to the heat of the day, his attitude was frosty, a complete one-eighty from the guy who'd rained kisses on her stomach this morning, placed his mouth between her thighs and rocketed her to an orgasm before she was even halfway awake. She'd opened her eyes to his satisfied smile, laughter in his amazing eyes...

She couldn't see his eyes now, but suspected that, behind his dark shades, they were the colour of pine trees in a blizzard. His expression was remote, his muscles tense, and his attitude screamed 'don't bother me'. Right now, he was, unfortunately, acting like the grown-up version of the young man she'd once known and been wary of...haughty, touchy, dismissive. Back then she'd always felt like a bug under his shoe, as if she weren't good enough to stand in his shadow, never mind at his side. It had hurt her badly; it now scalded and scorched her, to feel the same emotions from a man who she was, unfortunately, falling for.

So stupid, when she *knew* people didn't change.

Her breath caught at the back of her throat as she hurtled back to being a child, when she'd be hugged and then pushed away, sometimes in the same minute, by one of her parents. Where she'd be praised and then scolded, bolstered, then denigrated. Her life with her parents had been a roller coaster of emotions, and she'd never known what the truth was.

Farrell had been one person this morning but was someone completely different now. And that left her with a burning question…who was the real Farrell Wolfe? Was it the man who held her in his arms as he slept, who stroked her hair, who told her he loved having her in his bed and in his arms? Who kissed her nose when he delivered her morning coffee, who tested the temperature of the shower before allowing her to step inside the oversized cubicle? Or this man, cold, distant, unreachable? Snappy and silent?

Thea climbed to her feet. She couldn't do this, couldn't be with someone who blew hot and cold, who could be kind one minute, distant the next. It brought back too many terrible memories and made her feel too insecure. Fun sex, a warm, gorgeous body next to hers, weren't enough to risk the pain of being hurtled back into her painful past.

This was why it was better to be on her own…

Thea wrapped her sarong around her hips and plopped her floppy sunhat on her head. She picked up her flip-flops and started to walk away.

'Where are you going?'

She turned back to look at him. He hadn't stood up, nor had he made any effort to move. That said quite a bit, didn't it?

'I'm going back to the villa,' she told him simply.

'Why?'

'Because your company is so scintillating,' she murmured, at her sarcastic best.

Farrell rose and linked his hands behind his neck. Damn, when he did that, his biceps bulged and his core tightened, delineating his washboard abs. So hot…

No, she was mad at him and, worse, disappointed that he clearly felt he couldn't talk to and confide in her. And so frustrated for feeling this way. This wasn't, she told herself, a relationship;

it was a fling. Maybe it was time they stopped, because she couldn't handle him like this.

'I think it's time I moved into my own villa,' she said, sounding like a prim Victorian miss.

'For the love of all that's holy...' Farrell dropped his hands to his sides, but his shoulders remained up around his ears, his expression confused. 'I don't understand what's happening here,' he muttered.

Thea knew she was overreacting but couldn't stop herself from feeling ultra-defensive. A part of her knew he was grappling with something, and she was hurt that he couldn't, or wouldn't, tell her. The contrast between fun Farrell from earlier and distant Farrell now had her making comparisons between him and her parents. It wasn't fair, and she knew it. But maybe this was life's way of warning her to be careful. To slow down, to not allow herself to get emotionally involved. To step back.

She couldn't let herself fall for Farrell, or anyone. People weren't consistent, and she needed consistency more than she needed air to breathe. Consistency was safety...

She rubbed her hands over her face and released a long sigh. 'I'm sorry, I sound ridiculous. I am ridiculous. Blame it on the heat, on being a redhead in the sun.'

'That's not what this is about.'

No, of course it wasn't. It went far deeper than that, to the person—still needy, still insecure— she was deep inside. To the past and her parents, who, despite her not having spoken to them years, still, unfairly, affected her life.

Thea gestured to the path leading away from the beach. 'I'm going to go take a nap. I'm sure I'll feel more like myself later,' she said. 'You should go back to work. I know you have lots to do.'

She hurried up the sand to the stone wall that separated the beach from the resort's gardens and hopped over it, grains of sand falling off her feet as she hit the grass.

'Thea!'

She ignored Farrell's irritated shout and stepped onto the path, the stones hot from the heat of the sun. She yelped but didn't stop to slide on her flip-flops. She didn't want an excuse for Farrell to catch up, for them to continue their useless conversation.

Farrell assigning her a villa would tell her whether he wanted this to end or not. If he did that, she'd rather swallow glass shards than allow him to see that he'd hurt her. But what if he didn't? The smart thing to do, the safe thing, would be to move out anyway, to stop this craziness before it turned messier and more dangerous. Because if something as silly as him not talking to her could unsettle her, then falling for him and having to walk away would devastate her. So she repeated the mantra buzzing around her brain.

It's only sex. Nothing more, nothing less.

And prayed that she'd soon start to believe it.

Farrell found Thea sitting on the small beach of his private cove, the waves playing tag with her toes. He'd been worried when she hadn't arrived for supper with the rest of the guests earlier, and after checking with the resort manager on duty, he'd discovered she'd asked for a salad to be delivered to the villa. It was still in the fridge in his kitchen, untouched.

Her response to him earlier today still puzzled him, and he wanted to get to the bottom of her prickly behaviour—she'd reminded him, for the first time, of the spiky uni student she'd been. Yes, he'd been quiet, his mind full of how to handle the Vunilagi Sands resort scandal if it broke, but her reaction had been a little extreme. Had she been serious about wanting to move out of his villa? He didn't want her to go anywhere. Not, scarily, for the longest time.

He sat down on the sand next to her and pushed champagne glasses into her hands. She wore a long aqua maxi dress, and her hair picked up the oranges in the sunset, turning it more fiery than it normally was. He went to work on opening the bottle of cold champagne, shoving the plastic cover and wire into his shirt pocket.

'I thought champagne was only for celebrations,' Thea said as he gently eased the cork out of the bottle.

'I think champagne works just as well in a fight,' he replied, the cork leaving the bottle with a quiet plop.

'You didn't make it fly,' she stated, looking disappointed.

'Firstly, a flying cork would be a pain in the arse to find in this fading light, and secondly, a flying cork is often associated with flying champagne. This is a Ruinart Blanc de Blancs, far too expensive to waste.' He took a glass from her and poured the liquid gold into it. They swapped glasses, and Farrell pushed the bottle into a sand well and lifted his knees.

They'd had, well, it probably couldn't be called a fight…a communication breakdown would be a better description of what had occurred earlier. But he was still happy to sit on the sand next to her, saying nothing. He felt comfortable in her presence, as if he didn't have to fill the silence or be something he wasn't. He could just breathe.

Out of the corner of his eye, he saw Thea take a sip of the champagne, heard her soft sigh. 'It's nice.'

It was exceptional, but he wasn't going to quibble over her choice of words. Talking about words… 'I wasn't deliberately ignoring you earlier; I was just trying to work through something,' he stated. He knew she wanted details, but what could he say? That his father had raped the environment and conned uneducated people out of their land? That he'd done it in the name of corporate profits? And, despite trying really hard to make a difference, Farrell didn't think he'd ever make it right?

Thea crossed her legs and placed her glass on the sand next to her. She leaned back on her hands, her eyes on the ever-changing swathes of colours of the sky. He'd seen hundreds of sunsets, but every one was different, every one amazing.

'I became an emancipated adult when I was sixteen,' Thea said, her voice soft. 'From the moment my application was granted, I lived alone, ate alone, did everything alone. I supported myself, educated myself, raised myself.'

He stared at her profile, trying to make sense of her words. He didn't know much about the process but was pretty sure becoming an emancipated adult wasn't easily attainable. Standards had to be met.

'Why?'

She didn't look at him, and he could understand why. Sometimes it was easier to look away when you were talking about difficult subjects, easier not to see your emotions reflected in someone else's eyes. 'Somehow, the two most narcissistic, self-involved people in the world managed to find each other and fall in love. That being said, I'm not even sure if they are capable of doing that.' She waved her words away. 'Anyway, they each found the person who understood them best, who fed their worst instincts. Then they had me, and I was their personal, emotional plaything.'

He swallowed, feeling the rage building inside him.

'Their best game, the one they played most often, was keeping me on edge. Over the course of a day or two, sometimes three or four if they were feeling particularly mean—enough time for me to start to think they'd turned over a new leaf, that things were finally going to start to get better—they'd compliment me, tell me how wonderful I was, how smart, pretty, talented and how proud they were of me. Just when I started to enjoy the attention, when the wariness and distrust started to fade, just a little, they'd switch and tell me I was useless, and ugly, and stupid and how they wished I'd never been born.'

He heard the echoes of pain in her voice, threads of fear. He wanted to haul her into his arms but knew better than to touch her right now. Sometimes, you simply had to listen.

'Life with them was a constant roller-coaster ride, up and down, around and around. There were days when I thought I'd go mad,' she admitted. She picked up her champagne glass and downed the contents. 'I had to leave to save myself.'

He could understand that.

'I don't talk to people, Farrell.' She met his gaze, her fantastic eyes miserable. 'But I find myself talking to you, telling you things I've never told anyone before. For some reason, I trust you with my secrets.'

He winced and pushed a hand through his hair. How the hell was he supposed to respond to her confession? By telling her he trusted her with his own awful truths? The thing was—he didn't. He couldn't. Wouldn't let himself. And yet, he ached to confess, to let it bleed, just to ease the pressure in his chest. The temptation was maddening. The story of his past—his father's misdeeds, the life he took for granted, expected, the life funded by the pain of others, at the expense of land lost and fragile ecosystems—possibly, maybe, even a life!—pressed against his ribs, a volcano ready to blow.

But if he told her, if he admitted how deep the rot went, would Thea believe him? Or would she look at him and see only what everyone else did—his father's son, a whiny rich boy, unworthy, someone who was, essentially, empty?

'I want to, Thea,' he said, voice low, rough. And he did. He just didn't know how. Nor was he brave enough. It would be easier if he knew whether she'd accept or condemn him. But he couldn't. And he couldn't bear to gamble on the possibility that she'd walk away. So he'd do what he always did—lock it down, keep the mess inside, control the story before someone else did.

The divide between them was too wide, too dangerous to cross. And off this island? There was no chance. The outside world was louder, sharper, more merciless. He couldn't imagine them surviving it. But for now, they had hot nights, whispered laughter, and the illusion of happiness.

'Can we just be…you and me?' he asked, laying his hand on her thigh, searching her eyes. 'Because right now is all we have.'

She nodded, and when he lowered his mouth to hers, relief rushed through him. He could give her, and himself, this moment. No more, no less. Now was all he had to offer. It was all he deserved.

The next day, Farrell stepped into his office and nearly walked into Kyle. He sidestepped him.

'What are you doing hovering outside the door?' he demanded. He yawned: yet again, he'd had little sleep. But he had minimal time left with Thea, and he wasn't going to waste time sleeping. He could sleep later. Or when he was dead.

'Any chance of coffee?' he asked, raking his hair back.

'I asked the manager to let me know when you stepped into the lobby,' Kyle said. 'There's a jumbo-sized mug on your desk.'

Farrell frowned at him. They'd been together a long time, and Kyle wasn't usually this deferential. And he rarely greeted him with a cup of coffee and a frown. 'What's up?' he asked, his heart rate picking up. Why did he feel as if he were standing in the lights of an oncoming train, his feet glued to the rails?

Dread washed over him. 'Did the nursing home call?'

Kyle frowned. 'Your dad, as far as I know, is fine, Farrell.'

Thank God. Right. His father and his rapidly declining mental and physical health weren't something he needed to face today. Gesturing for Kyle to follow him, Farrell walked into their shared office and up to his desk. Instead of walking around to his chair, he reached across the desk to pick up his coffee cup and took a big, hot sip.

Yes. This.

He leaned back, his backside against the edge of his desk, and looked at his friend. Kyle looked a little grey and a lot worried. Rattled didn't begin to cover his expression.

'Just say it, Kyle.'

'It hit the papers this morning,' Kyle said, his voice low, 'and it's all over the Internet, spreading as we speak.'

'Fiji?' he asked, but somehow he already knew. The story about Vunilagi Sands had finally broken. 'Okay, we planned for this. Put out the press statements we prepared, get the PR department to do their thing.'

The remaining colour drained out of Kyle's face. 'You don't understand, Farrell. They have it *all.*'

All? What did that mean? My God, ice sliding into veins was worse than anyone could imagine. 'What do you mean?' he demanded.

'They have all the details about every dodgy deal your father made. This isn't only about Fiji; they are exposing the rip-offs in the Rockies, in Vietnam, in Zanzibar. Mexico too. They have everything.'

Farrell didn't hear the coffee cup crashing to the laminated floor below his feet; he barely noticed the hot liquid soaking the cuffs of his trousers, the sting of burned skin.

He'd expected, prepared for, one story, one scandal, not all of them. He'd expected a rocket, but this was a nuclear strike.

'The story about Wolfe International ripping off communities and destroying ecosystems is everywhere. And the way it's written makes it sound like it's happening now, and not decades ago. It's also highly detailed, impeccably resourced and, worst of all, completely convincing.'

It was here, the thing he most feared. A part of him was glad to finally face it, to get it out in the open. There was no chance of him or the company coming out of it unscathed; at best, they'd take a massive hit, at worst, the company's stocks would plummet, and investors would pull out. But he would deal with it, face it, and, when he was done, pick up whatever pieces remained and carry on. He wouldn't have to spend the next five or ten or twenty years looking over his shoulder, waiting for it to take a bite out of him. It was finally here, teeth bared.

It did, he admitted, have the potential to obliterate his world. But facing something was always better than not knowing where it was hiding, and how and when it would strike. He pulled in a deep breath. 'Okay. So, it's out. What do we do next?'

Kyle shook his head and rubbed his hand over his face. 'Shit, Farrell.'

'Don't panic, we can work our way through it,' he assured Kyle. If he didn't project confidence, everyone else would start to flounder, and that would make the situation a hundred times worse. 'It's not the end of the world and, if we play it right, it won't do too much damage.'

That was such a lie, and he was in a world of hurt right now. He was flailing, completely shell-shocked, but he knew he had to step up, be the leader, shine light on the situation. He couldn't fall apart; if he showed how truly panicked he was—the urge to run screaming out of the room was strong—nobody would get anything done. He *had* to keep it together.

'Who knows about this?' he asked.

'Who doesn't?' Kyle shrugged. 'As I said, it's everywhere, Farrell. Every news channel and online publication is carrying it.'

That meant Thea had seen it. Or would see it soon. 'I suppose that cutting off the Internet to the island isn't an option, right?' he asked, not completely joking.

Kyle managed a small smile. 'It would only be delaying the inevitable,' he said. He slid his hands into his pockets, his expression intensely worried. 'How do you think the journalists here, the ones who are meant to promote Petit Saphir, will respond?'

Who the hell knew? 'I don't know,' he answered him. 'If they dodge the subject, they'll be accused of ignoring the facts. Hopefully, they'll report on our green initiatives. Maybe they'll be able to pour a little water on what I expect will be an out-of-control wildfire.'

'I suppose it's too late to tell them about your restitution projects, how you funnel back your profits into a foundation to support affected communities? Your environmental work?'

His entire body tensed. 'That would be the worst thing to do right now,' Farrell said. 'I'll be accused of whitewashing the scandal, of trying to spin my way out of it, of covering up the company's misdeeds.' No, exposing the work he did would backfire spectacularly.

'You have to give some sort of statement,' Kyle insisted.

'Have the press office compile a release saying everything happened before I took control of Wolfe International. I hate to shove this on my father, but—'

'He was the person who greenlit those decisions, Farrell,' Kyle pointed out.

He couldn't argue with that. But his dad was uncommunicative, permanently disabled, and suffering from dementia. He didn't think it was fair to shift the blame onto him, to allow the world to take potshots at a man who couldn't respond or defend himself. Though at the time, when he'd confronted him, his father had brushed all his concerns away, telling him that his actions were a business cost and unavoidable. Unavoidable, his arse.

'Have them prepare the press release. One paragraph, saying that it all happened two decades ago, we sincerely regret it, and that I am deeply committed to being ecologically aware. Keep it short and sweet.'

Kyle didn't look convinced. 'It's not going to help,' he warned.

Oh, he knew that. He could call a press conference, read out a carefully constructed statement, but they'd gut him before he finished his first sentence. They'd twist every word and make it look as if he was doing what Wolfes had always done—smilingly charming, wriggling free of blame. He'd be painted as slippery, evasive, a man allergic to accountability.

The company, in some shape or form, would survive—it always did. Guests with bottomless wallets weren't going to cancel their six-star holidays over what they'd dismiss as a small, doesn't-affect-me environmental controversy. But his brand and image would take a hit, and that was far more concerning.

Damn it. A thousand thoughts screamed for attention, but only one rose above the noise: *What does Thea think? What does Thea feel?*

Because if she looked at him and saw his father's son instead of the man he was trying to be—if he saw disappointment in her eyes—it would gut him deeper than any headline ever could.

CHAPTER TEN

Later that day Thea had to track Farrell down, which made her angrier than she already was, so when she found him sitting on a rock at the end of the resort's beach, she was hot, sweaty and annoyed. And thirsty. Eyeing the cold beer in his hand, she stood on her tiptoes to snatch it from his him and sucked down half before wiping her hand across her mouth and handing it back. Not the most ladylike action in the world, but she was past caring.

He met her eyes, and his mouth turned up in a smile that didn't hold a hint of humour. 'I take it you read the article?'

'Of course I read the damned article!' she half shouted. 'Everybody here has read the article; everyone is talking about it!'

'So, dinner is going to be fun, then,' he commented, his expression deadpan. But Thea now knew him well enough to look beyond the surface, and she saw a flicker of pain, possibly panic, in his eyes. The fine lines fanning his eyes were deeper, and she couldn't see a hint of the dimple that appeared only when he felt relaxed. Oh, and his shoulders were up around his ears, and the muscles in his neck were piano-string tight. He was, internally, freaking out. Not without cause.

The article she'd read earlier was Richter-scale-ten bad.

'So, what are you going to do, Farrell?' she asked. She placed her foot on the boulder to climb up it so she could sit next to him. Farrell held out his hand and, with one quick yank, hauled her up the rock. She sat down, and he handed her the beer back, taking another one from the small cooler behind her. She peered inside. Along with two more cans of beer was a bottle of whiskey. Right, he'd come prepared to stay here and drink.

Frankly, she didn't blame him.

He shrugged and stared out to sea. 'My PR department prepared a brief press release saying it all happened so long ago, when Wolfe International was a different company under different leadership.'

That was true, it had been a different time and under different management. What his father had done was despicable, but, if it was managed correctly, Farrell could put a lot of daylight between himself and the past. 'And you're going to tell the world about the work you've done on Grande Saphir, right? We can do it before we leave tomorrow, so take us around there, show us the solar systems, the schools, the clinic with its small theatre. Allow us to speak to the locals.'

If only one or two of the journalists picked up on the story and ran with it, or even just added it to their pieces, it would go a long way to show the world that Wolfe International was a totally different company now than it had been.

'I'm not going to do that.'

Thea lowered her can of beer, not sure she'd heard him right. 'I'm sorry…*what*?'

He shook his head. 'I'm not going to hold up Grande Saphir and say, look at what a good boy I've been, look at what I've done. If I do that, the island would be inundated with tourists, and secondly, the press and our competitors will accuse me of spinning the story or trying to whitewash the situation. And it could also make me look even more guilty. That I only rehabbed the island because I was trying to make up for past sins.'

Was that what he was trying to do? Make up for what his father did? His father, not him… She picked his words apart and frowned. 'Wait, hold on, why are you taking responsibility for any of this?' she demanded. 'You were, at best, a teenager when your father pulled this crap. You had nothing to do with it.'

He wouldn't look at her, and Thea stared at his stone-like profile. 'I'm trying to understand why you feel guilty, Farrell. Why are you allowing the world to bash you when you have a very decent explanation?'

He crushed the empty beer can in his fist, the sharp crack of metal splintering through the air, then tossed it into the cooler and reached for the whiskey. The cap twisted off, and he lifted the bottle to his lips, taking a long, deliberate swallow. His throat worked, his jaw tight, his eyes still fixed on the horizon.

'I really don't want to talk about this, Thea, and it's got nothing to do with you.'

The words were flat, and oh-so-cold, merciless verbal bullets tearing through sinew and bone. She blinked at him, her chest heavy, her pulse tripping over itself. Hold on…*stop*. She was good enough to share his bed, to share his table, to laugh and kiss and make love with, but not enough to be trusted with his past and his pain? Not enough to be let in?

He knew—he had to know—that she'd noticed what he did for Grande Saphir. He'd spent so much money, given effort and time, and gone to lengths few CEOs ever would. She'd seen him. Yet, he'd still slammed the door in her face.

'I told you about my parents,' she whispered, her voice breaking. The waves mirrored her mood, swelling and restless, the wind whipping her hair across her eyes. A storm was brewing out to sea, and a hurricane rushed through her heart. She pushed her hair back with an unsteady hand. 'I told you how lonely it was. How I brought myself up. How I stopped depending on anyone because they always let me down. I opened up to you, Farrell. *You.* I never do that with anyone. And that's all you can say to me? That it's got nothing to do with me?'

He still didn't look at her. Neither did he flinch. Or even react. His gaze simply stayed on the churning sea.

'We're having a fling, Thea,' he said finally, each word clipped, hard. 'A fling doesn't mean I have to tell you stuff. We're almost done, anyway, so what's the point? I shouldn't have taken you to Grande Saphir. That was a mistake.'

She also heard what he didn't say—silent, but stunningly loud. *I made a mistake with you.*

She could sympathise with all those women he'd dated and dumped at uni; being dated and dumped was incredibly painful. For her it hit deeper, and pressed against old, deep bruises. She'd grown up with doors closing in her face— mostly with a slam—and now Farrell was doing it to her, too. Swept away by how much fun being with him was, she'd forgotten to protect herself…

And because the past had long claws, her parents' voices rose unbidden in her head… *We made a mistake having you.* How different was this, really? Different person, same wound. The pain was a tidal wave, crashing hard, and she almost couldn't breathe. Because she'd thought—believed—he was better than this. That behind the polish and the charm was a man worth knowing, worth trusting. That he wasn't like them. That he could be different. That she could be different with him.

'Please,' she said, her voice small and jagged and thick with a desperation she hated. 'Please… don't, Farrell.'

Don't be like them. Don't be another person who makes me regret hoping. Don't leave me trying to hold my shattered heart together.

Because if he did, he'd finish the work her parents had started.

Wanting to avoid a fight, or more hurt, she returned to his earlier statement. 'You are not responsible for what your father did, Farrell. You were a child; he made those decisions without your input.'

His eyes landed on her face, scorching through her. 'You have no idea what I did or didn't do, Thea. What I was and wasn't.'

'Then, talk to me, Farrell, help me understand,' Thea begged.

That was the one thing he couldn't, wouldn't do.

Farrell took another belt of his whiskey, enjoying the burn. It made a trail of fire down his throat, the only part of him that felt warm. Even though the temperature was in the mid-thirties, he felt cold from the inside out. The worst had happened, and what was it they said about walking through hell? You just had to keep on walking...

The exposé was mostly true; there were a few minor details they'd got wrong, but essentially, they were spot on. They had numerous sources, but Farrell suspected they were all people giving anecdotal evidence rather than physical documents. And without documents, Wolfe International couldn't be sued. They were, legally, in the clear.

Morally, he felt as if he were covered in slime. Should he have blown the whistle on the company back then? He'd buried the documentary proof; had it been the right thing to do? No matter how often he told himself that he'd had little choice, that his dementia-riddled father would never have coped in jail, that thousands of people around the world would've lost their jobs, that he wouldn't be able to make any financial restitutions if Wolfe International didn't exist—justice required big money and WI was a cash cow—he still felt...*dirty*.

He'd never be free of the stain.

Farrell looked at Thea's ashen profile, her bobbing throat. God, was that a tear sliding down her cheek? He placed his hand on his heart, wishing he could tell her his was on fire, that a knife was ripping his insides apart. Thea dropped her beer can in the cooler and wrapped her arms around her bent knees. 'What am I doing?' she softly asked. 'Why am I begging you to open up to me?'

He didn't know; she should've walked away two minutes into their conversation. She was so much better than he deserved.

'If I am going to be with someone, then I need him to be with me. Really be with me, and that means getting to know him, but you have a solid steel wall between your feelings, your past and your thoughts. If I am going to be vulnerable, then I need the man in my life to be the same.'

Farrell felt hot, then cold. He couldn't do that, be that. Being vulnerable, allowing someone close enough to hurt him, was his worst nightmare. Why not just hand her a scalpel and tell her to dissect him without any painkillers?

'I can see the horror on your face,' Thea said. 'I like you, Farrell, I do. Far more than I expected to. But I know we can't do this long term.'

God, it was one thing for him to think it, say it, but hearing Thea give up on them was gutwrenchingly painful. She stared out to sea, sadness flitting across her features. She turned to look at him and held her index finger and thumb an inch apart. 'I was this close to falling for you, about to slide down that slippery slope into love, but I won't let myself do that.' She shook her head. 'You're a nice guy, on the surface, and I love being around you. But as soon as something hard rolled in, you slipped back into who you used to be. Life isn't all tropical islands and sunshine, Farrell, and as lovely as this time has been, it's not real. Tough times are, and we show who we truly are when they come along.'

He heard the visceral pain in her voice, the wobble. 'But I love myself more than I like, or love, you, and I can't put myself in a situation that is so similar to my parents—'

He freely admitted that he was a jerk, but he'd never been mean to her. 'Hold on—'

'Let me rephrase that,' Thea interrupted him. 'I won't get on that "will he, won't he, what is he thinking and feeling?" roller coaster with you, Farrell. I won't get on that roller coaster with anyone.'

She stood up and, needing a reason not to look at him, shook out her dress. She looked as if she was about to walk away, out of his life. He didn't want her to leave, but he knew he couldn't ask her to stay. 'Thea—'

She gathered her hair and pulled it into a loose

bun and secured it with the band hidden by the bracelets on her wrist. 'I love your resort, Farrell. I do. I think you've created something special here. I'm super impressed by the work you did on Grande Saphir, and I wish you'd tell the world about it and your other projects. They would negate what Wolfe International did in the past—'

He sprang to his feet. 'Are you walking away, Thea?'

She cocked her head. 'Are you asking me not to?'

Yes, no… God. All he knew for sure was that he wanted to be with her but couldn't.

'That was a yes or no question,' she said sadly. 'And your non-answer is a no, Farrell.'

There was nothing he could say, and asking her to stay would be crass and supremely tactless. They'd run out of steam, out of road, completely out of options. There was nothing he could do, without insulting or hurting her further.

'I loved every minute of the time I spent with you, Thea,' he said, his voice low. He heard the crack in his voice, the longing leaking through, and wondered if she heard it too. 'I had so much fun with you.'

He caught the shimmer of tears, her grey eyes drenched with regret. 'Me too, Farrell.'

There was nothing more to say, nowhere else

to go. Thea looked around, blinked rapidly and gestured to the path leading up to the house. 'I haven't been here long but so much has happened. And I'm leaving tomorrow so I might as well go and pack. I'd like to stay in another villa tonight, my last night on the island. And if you could send someone to collect my bags, I'd be grateful.'

She belonged in his villa. It was where she needed to be…no, where he needed her to be. Feeling battered, Farrell rubbed his hands over his face. Thea hopped off the boulder and as she hit the sand, it scattered, sticking to her calves and feet, and the edge of the hem on her sundress. The setting sun deepened the red highlights in her hair and accentuated her gorgeous freckles. For as long as he lived, he'd remember Thea standing in the rays of the setting sun, the light turning her dress slightly transparent, her hair blowing in the wind.

She looked up at him, her expression sombre. 'I don't want to draw this out, but there's something else I need to say…'

Farrell braced himself, waiting for her to excoriate him.

'I don't know what happened back then, Farrell,' she said, her voice soft but determined. 'But I know something did, something that is still affecting you today. Something bad enough that you have regrets, something you feel that you can't come back from.'

Damn, she was perceptive. Or maybe she knew him better than he'd realised. Then again, hadn't she always seen below the surface layer he presented to the world?

'But I also know that whatever you did, you did it because it was the right thing to do,' she said. 'Maybe you were faced with two bad choices, or you were pushed into a corner, or you are protecting somebody or something. I know that you are blaming yourself.'

God. How? How had she worked that all out?

But she wasn't done yet. 'And whatever it was, you did what you thought you had to do,' she stated, with no hesitation. Her eyes met his, and he saw the belief in hers, the rock-solid conviction. 'I know you are better than who you pretend to be, that you are better than people think you are. You are so smart, and thoughtful and… deep.'

He shook his head. 'I was terrible to you at uni, Thea.'

'Yes, you were, but that was you then; despite what I said earlier, it isn't you *now*. You are better, and wiser, and so, so different from the person you were.' She held her hair back with both her hands. 'Trust yourself, Farrell. Trust how far you've come, and trust people to see it. Let the world know who you are now, today, without the trappings of the past.'

That wasn't possible…was it? But how he wished it were. He was so very tired, mentally, physically, emotionally.

What would it be like to love this woman? Truly love her? To be a 110% percent authentic with her, showing her the good, bad and ugly sides of himself? It would be… He searched for the word. Freedom. Joy. It would be somewhere he could relax. Home.

But none of that was possible.

Because when she walked away—when she got on that plane, or was back in London with its grey skies and busyness, away from this stupidly seductive island—her innate good sense would kick in. With some emotional and physical distance, she'd remember who he was. His father's son. Still that spoiled, entitled rich boy who'd never earned a thing except a reputation for wanting more.

Unworthy of the CEO title. Unworthy of the company. Unworthy of the fortune he'd been handed.

And absolutely, spectacularly, unworthy of her.

'I hope you manage to do that, Farrell. I hope you step into being the man you actually are, not the one you show to the world,' Thea said.

She gestured to the beach behind her, the bustle of the bar, the late afternoon swimmers, and the barefoot waiters carrying finger appetisers and today's signature cocktail. 'I'm going to go now.'

He nodded and watched Thea's slim frame walk away, and he didn't take his eyes off her until she stepped off his beach and out of his life.

The next day, a few hours before she was due to leave the island, Thea sat on the veranda of her barely used villa. After booting up her laptop, she opened the saved tab to a reputable online publication and once again clicked on the headline *'A Wolfe at the Door... An Exposé'*. Thea read the article again, this time without the haze of anger, slowly, precisely, taking in every word, making sure she understood the context, the history, every nuance.

After she was done, she sat back and sighed. It was a solid piece of journalism. The writer had done his homework, researched his subject and spoke to many sources, some of whom had worked for Wolfe International, people who were directly affected by WI's money, land and power grabs. Many people had been affected by the company's actions, and the journalist, after years of investigating, had presented a solid, unbiased account of what had happened over twenty years ago.

It was well established and accepted by both of them that Farrell had been an overprivileged idiot, but he wasn't responsible for anything that had happened back then. He wouldn't have thought of anything beyond which girl to ask out on a date or what car he wanted for his birthday. He'd probably had no idea what was happening in his father's company and wouldn't have cared.

But she knew, better than anyone else, what he gave his time and attention to these days. Thea did a quick online search but couldn't see any response from Wolfe International or Farrell himself, beyond a brief statement saying that Wolfe International was committed to environmental sustainability and that the company was under different management now.

The fact that Farrell wouldn't allow anyone to divulge his efforts to develop Grande Saphir, the funding of new schools and clinics and houses, was a disaster for the company. His ongoing silence had given rise to a series of spiteful articles saying he was nothing more than a spoiled heir, someone who didn't give a damn about poor communities, or the effect his developments had on the environment, and that he was only concerned about corporate profits. Why was he acting like a turtle who'd pulled its head back into its shell? His company had an excellent opportunity to counter the allegations, to show that they'd turned over a forest of leaves, but he refused to take it.

And why couldn't he have told her any of this? Why couldn't he say, *'Hey, my dad was an utter bastard at business; he conned communities and raped the environment.'*? It wasn't as if her parents were saints! They'd been so bad that she'd divorced them, for heaven's sake.

Thea rubbed her hands over her face, unable to understand why Farrell struggled so hard to open up, not only to her but to the world at large. He wasn't only the handsome, gregarious hotel owner, the exemplary host. He was also smart and thoughtful, a deep thinker and more sensitive than most people imagined. He'd grown up to be one of the best men she'd ever met, and she was completely in love with him.

Oh, crap. Why did she have to fall in love with him? But how could she not? How could she resist the man who spent his time and money on rebuilding a reef, diving with scientists to make the natural world a little better? Who'd taught her, or tried to teach her, to paddleboard, with humour and patience? Who'd watched sunrises and sunsets with her, who'd wiped the tears off her cheeks when she'd cried? Whose arms promised protection and a safe harbour?

Sure, he couldn't open up, found it difficult to talk, but he was nothing like the boy he had been, nothing like the man portrayed in the papers. Just as she wasn't the product of her parents, he wasn't a product of his father. He was far better than he was portrayed, and she was the only one who knew who he really was, who'd seen the man behind the mask.

But everything he'd told her about Grande Saphir and the reef rehabilitation was off the record, and she couldn't write about it without his permission. No matter how much she wanted to help him, no matter how she ached to show the world how he was trying to make up for the damage the company had caused, she couldn't write a word until he said so. And if he was muzzling his PR department, then there was not much chance he'd allow her to spill the beans.

Aargh, she hated having her hands tied.

Frustrated, she turned to looking at the photos of the island she'd uploaded, thinking she'd make a start on working out which ones to use on her blog.

She had so many choices: brilliant seascapes of the turquoise water, bold and streaky sunsets, the stunning lodge in the soft light of morning, another of it lit up at night. She scrolled through the images, stopping abruptly when she came across one of Farrell the day he took her to see his coral reef rehabilitation project. He stood at the yacht's wheel, squinting off into the distance, a slight smile playing on his face. His hair was tousled by the wind, and the sun danced on his bare back and shoulders. He looked casual, free, unburdened.

So different from the smooth, always-on man she routinely saw interacting with the journalists and his investors, playing the perfect six-star-resort-owning host. He was very, very good at coming across as genial and sociable, the life and soul of the party. But Thea now knew he was anything but.

At his core, he was lonely, isolated, and burdened. Definitely overworked. He was pushing himself for some unknown reason, and there was no space in his life for a life partner. Hell, she doubted there was space and time in his life for a lover, even a part-time or long-distance one.

Something was nipping at his heels, causing him to run at an always frenetic pace.

He couldn't keep up this pace for ever, and people, as she now knew, weren't designed to live their lives solo. They didn't always need a massive tribe. But everyone needed someone. Every person on earth needed a friend, a partner, someone to provide, not only support and love, but perspective, guidance, and a different point of view. Someone to say 'no' and point out flaws, someone to knock off the hard edges that shaped and formed personalities.

She needed someone, too. Needed a man to hold her when she felt lonely, to laugh with her, to listen to her. To tell her to stop being overly sensitive or critical, to stand firm when chaos reigned. Unfortunately, she wanted only Farrell; he was the only man she could imagine in her life. But he wasn't prepared to take that journey with her. She needed him, but he didn't need her.

What she'd told him about needing to love herself more was the truth. She'd fought too hard to rebuild herself, to risk slipping back to stand on the sidelines of someone else's life. She'd paid too high a price in tears, silence, and disappointment to be noticed only when Farrell was bored, or restless, or in need of a warm body. That wasn't enough for her. Not any more.

She wanted—no, deserved—to be seen. To have a partner with both feet in, emotionally and physically, an integral part of his life. Yes, maybe she was asking for too much too soon, maybe she was risking it all with her insistence, but she couldn't—wouldn't—settle for scraps. Not after everything she'd endured.

She looked at her packed suitcases, waiting at the door. This was going to hurt, she decided. But, as she'd learned, all hurt faded. It left scars, of course it did, but all scars could be tolerated, eventually. She'd survived far worse than the cuts this man would leave. But she still felt awful, like a hollowed-out shell…

Why did love and relationships always have to be so painfully complicated?

Outside, Farrell pulled up in front of Thea's villa in a golf cart and eyed her half-open front door. Leaning back, he stared down at his hands on the wheel, hands that had stroked her skin, combed her hair, held her face and her hands. Hands that missed her…

He missed her. It had been less than eighteen hours since she'd walked away from him on the beach, but every inch of him missed every fraction of her. His bed felt empty, hell, his life felt empty without her presence.

But no matter how many hours he spent lying awake, how many hours he spent thinking about how they could be together, there was no way he could give her what she wanted. He was a Wolfe, and evolved relationships, making women happy, giving them what they needed— space, acceptance, understanding and, crucially, time and the truth—wasn't in their wheelhouse. He had work to do, projects to fund, restitutions to make. There were still a few projects from his father's time that he hadn't got around to yet, that required a detailed investigation for him, through the foundation, to be able to make amends and restitution. There were communities to help, kids to educate, and ecosystems to be rehabilitated. It was all he could do.

He did, after all, have blood on his hands.

But he still felt it was imperative to keep his actions a secret from everyone but his top executives, who'd all signed NDAs. He didn't want to bring attention to the company's misdeeds or be accused of seeking glory for himself. Or for the very worst truth to be exposed, the ultimate price that was paid.

Farrell sighed and rested his forehead on his hands. He simply wanted to continue to do what he'd been doing for years, quietly. And the only way to do that was to tell no one, especially not a reporter.

Farrell stepped out of the golf cart and walked up to the front door, pushing an anxious hand through his hair. He needed to say goodbye to Thea, to thank her for the best ten days of his life, for being a bright light, for the laughter, the amazing sex. For the best conversations he'd had—both light and deep—ever. He owed her that. He owed her a goodbye.

Even if it ripped out his soul.

He knocked on the front door and stepped inside, his heart in his throat as Thea walked into the open-plan lounge from the outside deck, cradling her laptop to her chest. Their eyes collided, and Farrell bunched his fist to keep from walking over to her, the urge to bury his face in her neck overwhelming. It would've been easier if he'd never met her again. Because living without her—being without the joy she'd brought to his world—was going to be hell.

'Hi,' she murmured, sliding her laptop into her leather rucksack. He took in her long, white cotton trousers—he'd slid them down her hips last week—and remembered pulling that pink shirt aside to kiss her shoulder.

He cleared his throat and wrenched his eyes off her. 'Hi.' He gestured to her luggage. 'Is this all of it? I'll put it in the cart.'

'Have you been demoted to bellhop?' she asked, and he heard the forced jokiness in her voice. She, like him, was finding this hard.

'Something like that,' he said. He pushed his hands into his pockets. 'Are you ready to go?'

He saw her quick shake of her head, then the sad smile tugging at her lips. 'Mm,' she murmured, hitching her backpack over her shoulder.

'Are you flying back to London?' he asked, desperate to extend his time with her, even if it was only a minute. He was acting like a teenager who couldn't hang up the phone first, but he didn't care. He just wanted a few more minutes to commit everything about her—the way her hair turned a deeper shade of red when the light hit it, her crazy long eyelashes, each freckle on her nose and cheeks—to his internal memory bank.

She leaned her hip into the arm of the couch. 'Yes. I'll be there for a few weeks, then I'm due to head to the Gold Coast.'

'Long flight.' God, could he sound any more inane?

'I'm used to it,' she said. She pressed her fingertips against her forehead and, when she dropped her hand, her direct gaze pinned him to the floor. 'Why are we exchanging small talk, Farrell?'

He rubbed the back of his neck. She had a point; they were only drawing out the inevitable.

'Has anything changed?' she asked, and he picked up the slight wobble in her voice, the hint of hope. 'Can you let me in? Can you talk to me?'

He really wished he could. But it was impossible. He stared at a point past her shoulder. The sea had no right to look so pretty today, he decided. It should at least have the grace to look sullen or wild. How could the world still be bright and bold when his heart was cracking?

He wanted to say yes, promise her something he couldn't give, so he simply shook his head. Her face crumpled, just for a second, then she pushed her shoulders back and straightened her spine. Her eyes cooled, and the Thea he knew, bright and funny and compassionate, stepped behind a wall of professionalism. She, very deliberately, glanced at her watch. 'Shall we load my luggage?' she asked politely. 'I don't want to be the one who keeps the others waiting.'

Farrell nodded and turned to pick up her large suitcase, then the smaller one. He welcomed the slight burn in his biceps as he placed her baggage in the well of the cart, conscious of the ever-widening hole in his heart.

He slid behind the wheel and felt the space between them stretch. Farrell couldn't escape the truth clawing at his chest. Losing her felt as if he were drowning.

CHAPTER ELEVEN

IN HIS CANAL WALK OFFICE, Farrell turned, his shoulders relaxing a fraction when he saw it was Kyle who'd slipped through the door. After a series of brutal board and management meetings, where the will-not-die article was discussed ad nauseam, Kyle was the only person whose company he could tolerate right now. His and Thea's.

Farrell pushed away the memory of her lovely face as he half sat on his desk, pulled down his tie and loosened the top button of his shirt. It didn't help ease his tight throat; he'd started feeling as if he were being strangled in the Seychelles and, ten days later, the feeling had yet to dissipate.

Without Thea, his heart was also on life support, but he couldn't pay it any attention right now. He had a company to save, and with every day that passed with the story receiving top billing, his company took another faltering step backwards. It was teetering in the balance, and he needed to save it, but he was still underwater and drowning fast.

'Share price?' he asked Kyle, who looked as if he'd last slept a month ago. To be fair, they were both operating on minimal sleep, and they were both punch drunk.

'Plummeting.' Farrell appreciated Kyle's honesty because sugar-coating wouldn't help the situation. 'Also, it's started to affect our bookings; we've had a spike in cancellations and we need to think about whether we should refund booking deposits as a PR move.'

His eyes flew up. It was that bad? He dropped his head, silently releasing a series of creative curse words. It was blaringly obvious that he was running out of options. He could no longer con himself that waiting for the story to die down was an acceptable solution. If this went on for another month, hell, another week, the company would be in dire straits and would be close to impossible to save. It would also be ripe for a takeover, and he suspected that a few corporate sharks were already eyeing the situation…

It was, after all, what he would do if the shoe were on someone else's foot.

He lifted his head. 'What do I do?' he asked Kyle. He knew the answer already; he just needed his friend to voice the obvious.

'This is it, Farrell,' he replied, his expression

graveyard serious. 'You need to make one final decision…either tell the truth or let the company sink further.'

He rubbed his hands over his face. 'So, I go out there and tell them that I was protecting my dementia-riddled father, and that I hid company documents? That'll cause the share price to crash, and I'll be booted out as CEO of my own company.'

Kyle managed a small smile. 'As always, you're going too far. There are some situations when you only need to go halfway to the wall, not through it,' he stated.

Farrell frowned, not understanding. 'Explain.'

'You are one of the most brilliant people I know, so I cannot understand why you've been so resistant to use the easy solution right in front of your nose.'

'Just tell me,' Farrell growled.

'Open up about the foundation, show them what you've done, and how you've done it,' Kyle said, thankfully keeping his explanation simple. 'Show your plans for upcoming foundation projects. Show people, don't tell them, about the concrete actions you've instigated, over the years, to right the wrongs of the past.'

He didn't want to do that, didn't want the foundation's work being tainted by this scandal. It was his baby, the one thing he was completely, utterly proud of, the one thing he'd got oh-so-right. 'Keeping it apart, keeping it safe, is all that matters.'

Kyle scowled at him. 'That's crap! Your company matters! The people you employ, your suppliers who rely on Wolfe International to keep their people employed, matter, too. You've put so much time and effort into Wolfe International over the past decade and more, but you're prepared to let it slip away because you want to protect the foundation. That's crazy talk, Farrell, and you're not a crazy man.'

Unfortunately, Kyle was not done with him yet.

'And if WI fails, how is the foundation going to keep going?' he demanded. 'Where is it going to get the bulk of its funding from?'

Farrell stared at him, his words landing and, for the first time, registering. He'd had years of experience negotiating at the highest tables in the land, for hundreds of millions, but he'd failed to connect two and two. Without Wolfe International, there would be no Wolfe Legacy Foundation. The two were bound, intertwined. He needed the foundation to give his life meaning, the foundation needed money to survive... It was a symbiotic relationship.

He sank to his haunches in front of his desk and stared at the floor beneath his designer shoes. Without Wolfe International, the foundation would turn up its toes and die. And without Thea in his life, he would shrink, too. Oh, he wouldn't die, but he'd wither away, becoming less and less himself, more of the Wolfe International CEO and less authentic.

He was in the middle of a crisis, and he was thinking about Thea? Maybe it was because he missed her with the power of a thousand suns—pathetic, but there it was. Or maybe it was because she'd said the same thing to him before she'd left Petit Saphir. She'd told him to go public with the foundation, to let people see the work he'd done on Grande Saphir. She'd even offered to document it for him.

And he'd shut her down. But if he could just open up to the world about his actions and his values, about how much he valued the natural world and how committed he was to making up for his father's failings, he—*maybe*—could have the company *and* the foundation. And with a little breathing room and everything out in the open, he could finally be more himself.

But what did it all mean without Thea? She was his brightest light, his North Star, the person he most wanted to be with. Somehow, underneath the hot Seychelles sun, he'd fallen in love, properly, authentically in love. The real him loved the real her. And he couldn't imagine another day without her.

But he'd have to because, before he went to Thea, hoping for a new start, a new life, he had to salvage his company and pull it back from the brink. He needed a plan, and, since he'd silenced his extremely expensive, massively talented PR department, he thought he'd better start there.

He looked up at Kyle. 'Call a meeting with the PR department. I want everyone there, from the director to the interns. We're going to need all hands on deck.'

Kyle's huge, relieved grin chased away his tiredness, and Farrell realised it was the first time he'd seen him smile since before they'd left the Seychelles. He returned his smile, and it felt strange, as if his muscles had forgotten what to do.

'So, are we going to fight fire with fire?' Kyle asked, cocking his head.

Farrell grinned from where he still squatting on the floor. 'No. We're going to fight fire with a flamethrower the size of Texas. And a whole lot of gasoline.'

Farrell asked her to meet at the Bookish Bar, a smart bar close to his office. Standing in the doorway, Thea watched him fiddle with the knot of his tie and pull down his suit's waistcoat. With his hair styled off his forehead, his stubble carefully trimmed, and his expression enigmatic, he looked like what he was, the high-powered CEO of an international group of hotels. She hadn't expected to see the man she'd slept with in the Seychelles, but this corporate version of Farrell was a little unrecognisable.

But what did it matter? This wasn't a meeting to discuss their relationship, to see if there was any chance of them moving forward, or to find a way for them to be together. No, this was, as his text message had so briefly stated, a meeting about how she could help rehabilitate Wolfe International's reputation. Yes, she was happy to help him do that—she loved him, and she hated the situation he was in—but was it so hard to smile at her, to exude a little warmth?

Thea wished she'd worn something other than dark skinny jeans, a plain cream jersey and a leather jacket. She wished she'd pulled her hair back, done more with her make-up... She felt exposed. But Farrell, as he gestured for her to take a club seat opposite him, looked cool and composed.

He signalled to the waiter and asked her what she wanted to drink. Thea ordered an espresso, thinking she needed a caffeine boost to supercharge her alertness. When the waiter walked away, with an order for two double espressos, she leaned back and crossed her legs. Farrell leaned forward, rested his arms on his thighs and linked his hands together. Up close, she noticed the violet smudges under his eyes and his gaunt cheeks. He'd lost weight, and his face looked a little pasty. He was a man on the edge.

There was no point in exchanging small talk, so she jumped straight in. 'Why did you ask to meet me, Farrell?' she asked, keeping her voice low.

He looked at her, and she caught a brief flash of emotion in his eyes. Regret? Want? Lust? Then it faded, and a deep green curtain fell, stopping her from seeing into his soul.

'I need your help, Thea,' he said, somehow sounding both sad and irritated. He clearly hated being in this situation, hated having to ask her, or anyone, for help.

'Okay. What do you need?' she asked, her heart thumping. She had an idea of what he was about to say next, but she wondered how he'd frame it. Would he downplay the situation he was in, or give her some idea how far he was underwater? Would he tell her the truth?

'I'm in a world of hurt, and my company is even worse,' Farrell said, rubbing his hands down his face. Well, that was more honesty than she'd expected. 'I thought I could ride this scandal out, that it would die down a lot sooner than this, but I couldn't, and it hasn't. In fact, it's only getting worse.'

She'd been following along, and every day she winced at what appeared online. Because she loved him, she worried about the effect it was having on Wolfe International. And, naturally, on him. She had been, still was, so concerned about him. Judging by the way he looked right now, his tight shoulders and grim mouth, his exhaustion, she'd been right to worry.

'I need to turn it around and I need to do it fast,' Farrell told her.

He was finally taking action, and she was glad to hear that. But it might be a case of too little, too late. 'What do you need me to do?'

He jerked, then frowned. 'Just like that?'

She loved him; of course she'd help him. She'd do pretty much anything for him…anything legal, that was. 'Just like that,' she assured him. When he still looked unconvinced, she leaned forward and gripped his hand, sliding her fingers into his. 'Tell me what you want me to do, Farrell.'

'Aren't you going to ask me about the past, demand an explanation, ask for reassurances?' he questioned.

Thea sighed. He wasn't used to someone taking him at his word, wasn't accustomed to someone having complete faith in him. But he'd forgotten that she'd seen him in action, had been allowed to look, just a little, beyond the corporate CEO and owner to the man beneath the mask. She'd seen him gently place corals on the reef, talk to the locals on Grande Saphir, the honest, open way he interacted with his staff, and seen his love for the natural world. She saw him, clearly.

'No,' she calmly told him. 'Tell me how I can help you, Farrell.'

Because she would if she could. He might not love her, but her love wasn't conditional; it wasn't something she could give away and then retract when he didn't return her feelings or dance to her tune. Love didn't work that way.

Farrell stared at her for a few seconds, disbelief crossing his features. Then he shook his head and tapped the table with his index finger. 'My PR department is working on a statement, telling my side of the story, revealing to the world what my foundation has done and achieved.'

'Your foundation?' He'd briefly mentioned a foundation but hadn't gone into any detail. She sighed. Typical Farrell.

'The company makes regular payments to my Wolfe Legacy Foundation,' Farrell said, his tone brisk. 'I created the foundation to invest in the communities and environments where we build our resorts. It's also funded projects in places where, frankly, we did real damage—just as the article pointed out. It's my way of…' he hesitated '…trying to make amends for the pain WI caused in the past.'

He cut the air with a sharp wave of his hand, swatting his words away. 'I can't get into that right now. I don't have the time. The truth is that I can put out press releases for days, tell them what we are doing, what we've done, but I don't know if it will turn the tide. We need to show the world what we've been up to. And that's where you come in.'

She knew where he was going without having to say anything. 'You want me to write a piece about what I saw on Grande Saphir.'

'And the reef restoration project.' He nodded. 'I know I said it was off the record before, but I'm putting it on the record, and asking you to write about it, to get the word out there.'

Thea nodded. 'I can do that.'

She saw the relief on his face, saw his shoulders rise and fall. 'Thank you.'

He looked at her, hope and impatience in his eyes. 'When do you think it will be ready?' He rubbed his forehead with his fingertips. 'Damn, I know I sound pushy, but I don't have any time to lose. Is there any chance of you writing it tonight, posting it online by the morning? That way, my PR department can start promoting the hell out of it.'

Thea's eyebrows rose. 'You do know that it normally takes a week for me to write an indepth article like that? Especially if I want to get it right, if I want it to make a real impact. And, because it's so important, it needs to make a serious impact, Farrell.'

He pushed his hand through his hair, obviously frustrated. 'I know, I know, but I don't think I have a week left, Thea. It might be too late by then.' He linked his hands behind his head, and the curtain in his eyes fell away, revealing his desperation. 'You're my last shot.'

Well, then. It was a good thing she had an ace up her sleeve. She smiled and tapped the rim of her coffee cup. 'Actually, I already wrote the article. I finished it two days ago. I've been trying to find the courage to send it to you, to see if you wanted to use it.'

It took him a moment for her words to make sense. 'You've already written it?' he clarified, hope warring with the uncertainty in his voice, as if he wasn't able to believe his luck.

'Mm, I knew you needed something to counteract the attacks, but I couldn't post it without your permission.' Thea leaned forward and waited for his eyes to connect with hers. 'It's a good story, Farrell—no, it's a great story. It would be a great story even without the scandal. It's what people want to read: a bright light in a dark tunnel.'

He looked completely shocked. 'I can't believe…are you being serious?'

Thea pulled out her phone and swiped her thumb across the screen. She opened her email account and looked at him, her eyebrow raised. 'What's your private email address?' she asked.

Farrell gave her the address, she accessed the document from her cloud and sent it to him. A few seconds later, his phone beeped with the incoming notification. 'There you go,' she said. 'I hope you are happy with it, because I honestly think it's one of the best pieces I've ever written.'

Farrell pulled out his phone, checked the message and closed his eyes. 'Thank you,' he murmured. 'I'm so grateful.'

She wanted his love more than his gratitude, but that wasn't going to happen. They were just an island fling, never to be repeated. They couldn't work in real life. 'Read it over, check it for inaccuracies. If you are happy with it, I can upload it and promote it through my social media channels. I will need some photographs of Grande Saphir, so can you email me some? Preferably in high res.'

Farrell nodded, still looking dazed. 'Yes, of

course.' He shook his head. 'I can't believe how easy this was.'

She wanted to tell him how she'd felt compelled to write that article—how she'd stayed up night after night, drafting and redrafting, chasing accessibility and impact. She'd laboured to find the precise mixture of humour, emotion and facts, so her words might resonate, would matter. She wanted him to know she'd poured herself into it, even without the certainty that he'd ever read it, let alone use it.

The hours, the exhaustion, the jittery over-caffeination, the endless cycle of starting again and again—it had cost her a little piece of her soul. And yet, she knew she'd do it all over in a heartbeat. Because it was all she had to give him.

That…and her love.

At the time, neither had seemed enough. It was obvious he still wasn't interested in the latter.

He tugged at his collar, fiddled with his tie. 'My father…' He hesitated. It was strange to see the usually so confident Farrell sounding off kilter. 'He wasn't a nice man. I wasn't either.'

Thea frowned. What was he getting at? He couldn't actually believe he and his father were cut from the same cloth—could he? Thea was about to ask him to explain when his phone dinged again, and he looked down at it, his brow furrowing. 'I need to go,' he said, and Thea wondered if she'd imagined the regret she heard in his voice. His eyes met hers, and Thea wondered if this was the last time she'd look into them, sit opposite him. It was highly likely. 'I'm sorry, but…'

But he had a company to save, a PR campaign to launch. Thea swallowed her bitter disappointment. A part of her had foolishly hoped for…

She'd hoped for more. 'Check the article and send me the photographs. As soon as I get your go-ahead, I'll upload it,' she told him.

He pushed to his feet. 'It'll be soon. Within the next hour or so. It's my highest priority.'

Thea looked away, hoping he didn't see the sheen of tears in her eyes. Her story was his highest priority, but she wasn't. She never would be.

Farrell rested his hand on her shoulder and dropped a gentle kiss on her head. 'I hate to cut and run,' he murmured. He did, to his credit, sound regretful.

'But you have important things to do,' Thea replied. It took all her willpower to pull up her brightest smile and wave him away. 'Go.'

He looked down at her, and Thea fought the urge to hug him. When had he last been hugged, or told that someone was on his side? She knew she shouldn't, but the urge to touch him, one last time, was overwhelming. Standing, she pushed her arms under the sides of his suit jacket and wrapped them around his hard waist. Resting her head on his chest, she hugged him, trying to convey, through her touch, that she was on his side, that he could do this.

That he was loved. Even if he didn't want or need her or her love.

He stiffened, and she knew he wanted to pull away. Then, surprisingly, he released the smallest groan and pulled her into him, his arms wrapping around her, holding her so close a piece of paper couldn't come between them. He smelled gorgeous, but she missed the overlay of sea, the hint of sun she remembered from Petit Saphir.

He buried his face in her neck, and Thea felt his lips kiss her skin, so softly she wasn't sure if she'd imagined it. Then he loosened his arms and pulled back. He kissed her temple, murmured another low 'thank you' in her ear and strode away.

Out of her life. But never, she suspected, out of her heart.

CHAPTER TWELVE

FOUR DAYS LATER, Thea walked onto the veranda of her bungalow and took in the Pacific Ocean, just a few feet from her temporary home. She was in the Whitsunday Islands, the Australian sun was shining, and the ocean was a bright blue. There were more white beaches, with soft sand kissed by warm water. Rainforest-clad hills tumbled down to meet the tide. The brochures said this was the place where time slowed, where the air seemed cleaner, lighter, infused with salt and sunlight.

She'd heard the PR a thousand times before.

Thea couldn't help wishing this assignment had been a ski lodge or a jungle retreat. Being here, on another tropical island, without Farrell seemed wrong. To be fair, being anywhere without Farrell felt wrong. She looked over her shoulder to where her phone lay on the pristine white cover of her huge double bed.

Nothing new would've been posted since she'd last checked it five minutes ago. In contrast to the past few weeks, the groundswell of support for Farrell and Wolfe International was now unabated, and she knew her article had played a big part in rehabilitating his and his company's reputation.

He was now being called, by the press and public—both as fickle as hell!—modest and self-effacing for not immediately wanting to publicise his good deeds and was being held up as the example of how CEOs should address development in the face of climate change. He had been labelled 'an innovative and groundbreaking young leader'. Soon after her article had landed online, the company shares had started to climb again and they were now higher than ever.

He'd been avoiding the press and hadn't given any personal interviews, preferring to let his PR department and her article speak for him. Thea thought that was the right call; he'd been right to show, not tell. On a personal level, she wondered if he was eating properly, sleeping better, if he'd managed to go outside and get some fresh air. Since receiving a barrage of photographs of Grande Saphir from him, she hadn't heard from him. He'd gone radio silent. To be honest, Thea wasn't surprised.

They were done. Their fling was over, and there was nothing left between them but the memories of island-based laughter, a couple of deep conversations and spectacular sex.

But she missed him. She thought she always would…and she'd always ache when she visited white-beach island getaways reeking of romance.

Walking down the wooden steps leading to the beach, she sat on the second-to-last step and pushed her feet into the still-warm sand. The sun dipped beneath the horizon, tossing pink and purple streaks onto the sky. It wasn't as vivid as the sunsets in the Seychelles; somehow, it seemed a little muted and not as glorious.

Then again, everything in her world appeared less colourful. Nothing tasted as good as it did before she went to Petit Saphir, nothing smelled as strong as it had. It was as if she'd been dialled down…as though someone had applied a sepia-coloured filter to her life.

Thea picked up a shell and examined it, thinking she needed to head over to the lodge and grab something to eat. Her appetite was also muted, and she'd lost some weight. But the thought of food didn't appeal. Nothing much did.

She'd get over him, she promised herself. She would. She'd learned to live without her parents, had managed to live quite successfully on her own for a long time now. At some point, she'd be fine. She just didn't know when…

Thea felt something cold nudge her shoulder, and she spun around, seeing the wide green glass bottom of a bottle. Her eyes travelled up slowly. The label indicated it was a French champagne and the hand holding it was all too familiar. She recognised those fingers, the expensive watch on that strong wrist, the haphazardly rolled-back cuffs of his shirt. Unable to speed up her gaze, she took in his navy shirt, the V of tanned skin at his strong neck. Holding her breath, she looked at his stubble, that sexy mouth. She couldn't handle his eyes, not right now, so she skipped over them to take in his messy, windblown and finger-streaked hair.

Farrell was here. What in the world…?

She swallowed, then did it again. 'Uh… what…how?'

'Are you going to meet my eyes sometime soon, Thea?'

Thea gripped the edge of the wooden step, and her eyes collided with his. She'd never seen them warmer, nor less sure. Open, vulnerable, mesmerising. He smiled, and the lines at the corners of his eyes deepened. God, he was sexy. But was he real? She'd been thinking about him so much that it was highly possible he was a figment of her imagination.

His calf was within touching distance, so she reached out and gripped some leg hair and tugged. Farrell released a satisfying yelp, enough to convince her she wasn't hallucinating.

'Ow! What was that for?' he demanded. He placed the champagne bottle and two flutes on the lowest step and rubbed his calf, wincing.

'I thought I was imagining you,' she admitted. She looked at the bottle and glasses. 'Why do you have champagne? And why are you here? How did you *know* I was here?'

'Move up,' he ordered her and, when she did, he moved the champagne and glasses and sat down in the space next to her, his big shoulder pushed into hers, their hips and thighs aligned. 'To answer your last question first…you told me you were coming to Australia, remember? And then you put a post up on social media saying you were here. Once I knew that, it wasn't hard to track you down.'

'Okay, but that doesn't explain *why* you're here,' she replied, feeling confused. And turned on. Farrell in a three-piece suit was something, but Farrell in a half-open shirt and board shorts, and bare feet, was her favourite look. How was she supposed to make sense of anything when all she wanted to do was to put her mouth on his and kiss him senseless? The sun was warm, the sky and sea blue, the palm trees were swaying… how was she supposed to resist?

She jerked back as another thought hit her.

Was he just here for another island fling? Was this what would happen going forward? A series of hot island flings? The thought was incredibly depressing.

'I came to thank you, Thea.'

She flinched at his words. That was even worse. She wanted his love, not his thanks. 'You could've sent me a note,' she muttered.

'Mm, I could've done that, but I had more to say than just that. But, from the bottom of my heart, thank you.'

She turned to look at him and sucked in her breath when he lifted his hand to tuck a strand of hair behind her ear. His fingers trailed over her cheek and jaw, and she closed her eyes at the heat in his gaze. She knew he wanted her, but it wasn't enough. She wasn't prepared to settle for less than everything.

'You are so beautiful,' he told her, his voice rough. 'And you smell so good.'

Thea forced herself to pull her face away from his hand. She needed to change the subject, so she grasped onto the events of the past week. 'Wolfe International seems to be over the worst of it,' she commented, wrapping her arms around her bent knees.

'We are, thanks to you and your amazing article,' Farrell agreed.

She'd written nothing but the truth; she'd simply told the world about Farrell's softer side and his commitment to the natural world and the communities he interacted with. 'I just told it like it is,' she said.

She felt Farrell's shoulder lift and fall. 'And if I'd explained sooner, it would've saved everyone a lot of grief,' he admitted.

She'd always wondered why he'd been so desperate to keep it a secret. 'Why didn't you?' she asked, curious.

It took him a while to respond. He rested his folded arms on his knees and stared out to sea. 'Like I said when we last met, my father wasn't a nice man. He cared about his image—his name, his power, the money, the influence. And I grew up thinking I was better, smarter, untouchable, just because I was a Wolfe of Wolfe International. Nobody ever told me no. I was ridiculously privileged and too oblivious to see it. I thought the world spun for me—and I never bothered to notice anything outside my bubble. At uni, I thought you were ridiculous for paying attention to human rights and climate change, and I thought your advocacy was pointless.'

Yeah, she knew that; she'd been there.

'But even back then, you made me feel uncomfortable, like you could see through me, that you knew I was a miserable human being, that I was soulless.'

He'd been young and spoiled, but calling himself soulless was a bit harsh. Before she could say anything, he continued.

'I was selfish and irresponsible. Because I have an eidetic memory, I never had to work hard or be accountable. Then when I left uni, I went straight to work at Wolfe, was immediately installed in a corner office and handed the power to lord it over people who had decades more experience and learned knowledge than I did. No prizes for guessing why we lost many of our most experienced executives that year.'

Thea knew that if she showed any emotion, she'd lose him, so she simply gestured for him to continue. He rubbed the back of his neck. 'I've never told anyone what I'm about to tell you, Thea.'

She bit her lip, her heart hammering in her chest. 'Okay,' she murmured.

'One year, a couple of years after I joined Wolfe, a man appeared on the pavement outside our office block. He held a sign, saying that Wolfe International had destroyed his community, scattered his people, and robbed them of their land and dignity. I, like everyone else, ignored him for those two weeks he was there. I knew he'd disappear soon, so I didn't give him much thought.'

He stared at his feet, and Thea knew he was

battling to find the words. He swallowed, and when he spoke again, his throat sounded as if it were full of gravel. 'He left, and life went on. Then, one November two years later, I was leaving the office… I remember it was one of those grim winter days, with icy, incessant rain. I nearly ran into her, a tiny woman, but quite beautiful, holding the same placard as the man had. I'm ashamed to tell you that I thought she was hot, so I persuaded her to have a cup of coffee with me at a café opposite our building.'

He sighed. 'I was about to go on a charm offensive, and then I noticed that her eyes were so big in her thin face, and she looked incredibly sad.'

'What did you do?'

'Something very out of character for me at the time,' he admitted. 'I ordered her a hot meal and an even hotter cup of coffee.' He pushed his hand through his hair. 'I suddenly needed to know how they were connected, his story. Hers.'

Thea placed her hand on his back and rubbed gently. 'Can you tell me?' she softly asked.

'He was from Fiji, from the same village my father had ripped off, the one that's at the centre of the article. He was a young teenager when his family, his friends and neighbours lost everything because of my father. Most of them had to relocate, to move to bigger towns to find work and start again.'

He looked at his hands. 'The man, Peni, managed to find a job, and he saved, for years, to buy a ticket to come to London to protest Wolfe International's treatment of his community. We didn't let him into the building and when he returned to Fiji, he died when his motorcycle hit a tree. The police ruled it an accident, but the family believes he took his own life, because he was depressed when he returned from the UK. His sister blamed us, rightly, for her brother's death, and she said the emotional pain of seeing everything he valued—his home, his traditions and his community—destroyed had caused him to take his own life. She took the money she'd saved to go to uni to travel over here to protest in the same way he did. It was her way of honouring him.'

He rubbed the back of his neck, and she felt his shudder. 'I wanted to walk away from her, but my feet were nailed to the floor. I wanted to refute and dismiss her words, but I couldn't. I felt sick at what they went through, the impact of my father's greed. I didn't want it to be true, mostly because I didn't want anything to change. So, I went back to the office and accessed the company system. As my father's son, I had the clearance to go deep.'

'And you discovered she was telling the truth?'

His eyes looked haunted. 'I also discovered her community wasn't the only one that had been annihilated by my father's greed. There were others, as the world now knows.'

Thea bit her lip but kept her hand on his back as silent encouragement. 'I confronted my father, and we had a massive fight. During it, he asked why I even cared. I was living well thanks to the decisions he'd made, and I had everything I wanted or needed. I'd never cared about anything or anyone before and was totally self-absorbed. So why did I now care about a group of people halfway across the world? Hearing that from him rocked me. His words made me look at who I was, and who I wasn't. It led, much to my father's regret, to a permanent shift in my attitude.'

She couldn't believe he was telling her so much, but she didn't want him to stop. She wanted to know it all. She rested her temple on his shoulder before kissing his biceps. 'Get it out, Farrell. Tell me everything.'

Not only because he needed to say it but because she needed to understand. They needed to be honest with each other to be able to go forward.

'Over the next couple of months, I harassed him to make restitution, to engage with the communities, to do something to atone for the damage the company had caused. He dug in his heels, said he wouldn't, and the rift between us grew wider and wider. I threatened to resign, and he told me to go. He told me that if I did, he'd disinherit me, that he'd no longer speak to me. After our last vicious fight, I left him in his office and went out and got drunk.'

Farrell closed his eyes and sighed. 'He had a stroke that night. A minor one, but it was enough to keep him out of the office for a few weeks. I stepped up, he returned to work, and we worked together for another six months, in an uneasy truce. But I knew something wasn't right; he was behaving erratically, forgetting key details, making strange decisions. I finally persuaded him to get tested, and he was diagnosed with early onset dementia.'

No matter what they'd done, nobody deserved that. 'Oh, Farrell.'

'He was adamant that he didn't want anyone to know, that he'd rather die than have people pity him. He started retreating from his friends and his colleagues, but he wouldn't step down as CEO. And his decisions went from bad to worse. I confronted him and, being my dad, he struck a deal. He'd step down, wouldn't cause a fuss, if I buried the shady deals. He demanded that I shred all the documents and that I pretend it never happened. If I did that, he'd transfer his shares to me, retreat to the south of France and retire quietly. And when the time came, he agreed he'd go into a care home. That's where he is now.'

His sad eyes slammed into hers, and Thea noticed his shoulders were up around his ears. 'The company was floundering, Thea, and if I didn't step in, it was doomed. Thousands would've lost their jobs. And, by doing that, I had the opportunity to reinvent WI, to take it in a new direction. I could also generate funds for a foundation and make some restitution to the communities we'd harmed. If I couldn't help one of them directly, if we'd destroyed it to the point it couldn't be rebuilt, then I helped an adjacent community.'

Why was he trying to convince her? She knew he was a good guy, trying to do the right thing. 'I get it, Farrell. You were faced with making hard decisions, and you took the path where the least amount of people would get hurt.' She thought about the articles that had been released and remembered that there was no mention of where his father was now, and she asked him about it.

Farrell shook his head. 'If anyone asked, and they have, I instructed the PR department to answer that he lives a secluded life and has no interest in the business. He hated the idea of anyone knowing he had dementia, and I'm honouring his request to keep it a secret.'

That was understandable. He was still his father, after all.

'So, that's it,' Farrell said, spreading his hands out. 'That's what happened.'

It was a lot, but it wasn't everything. She scooted back and half turned to face him and waited for him to look at her. 'When are you going to stop punishing yourself, Farrell?'

His eyes widened in surprise. 'I…what?'

'Yes, you were an overprivileged jerk. But you didn't make any of the decisions that harmed the communities and the environment. You have actively tried to do damage control, and have, in my opinion, done more than anyone could have expected of you. When are you going to let yourself be happy?'

He stared at her and cradled her cheek in his hand. He closed his eyes and rested his forehead against hers. 'Now, today. That's why I'm here, Thea.' He pulled back, and Thea fell into his eyes, so green, so intense. Before she could speak, he brushed his lips against hers, softly, reverently. Then his thumb drifted over her cheekbone. 'You're my happy, Thea. You're everything I want and need going forward.'

He was saying the words, but Thea didn't think she was understanding him correctly. 'You want me in your life?' she asked, confused.

'You *are* my life, Thea.' His fingers brushed

her hair away from her face, gently and reverently. 'Yes, I now understand I'm not to blame, that my father's decisions were not mine, and that I can't change the past. But I can make my future better and brighter, and to do that, I need you.' He smiled at her, and she caught the flash of his shallow dimple. 'I love you. You make my whole life better; you make *me* better.'

Right. Wow. Was this a dream? She reached out to pull his leg hair again, but Farrell anticipated her move and swung his legs away. He laughed, his eyes dancing with humour. 'It's not a dream,' he told her, capturing her hands in his and linking their fingers.

Okay. Well. Thea stared at him, her heart pounding. Could this really be happening? Was she going to spend the rest of her life with this person? Could she? A lick of panic coated her mouth.

'I promise not to put you on a roller coaster, Thea,' Farrell told her, reading her mind. 'I will never lift you to drop you, play with your emotions, or gaslight you. Are we going to fight?' He shrugged. 'Probably, occasionally. But we'll fight clean and we'll come out the other side better and stronger and more in love.' His eyes widened, and he scratched the side of his neck. 'Uh, that is…if you love me back.' Terror crossed his face and jumped into his eyes. '*Oh, my God.* I don't know if you do.'

A tiny giggle, more of a snort, escaped. He looked so adorably confused and uncertain. 'Of course I love you, Farrell,' she told him, her fingers on his hard jaw. His eyes lightened, a relieved smile lifted his lips, and he leaned forward to kiss her. She pushed her hand up between them and rested her fingers on his lips, wrinkling her nose. 'There's one little problem, though.'

He jerked back and frowned. 'What? What's the problem?'

She tipped her head back, gesturing to the cabin, and grimaced. 'It's small, horribly romantic and, crucially, there's only one bed.'

His dimple deepened, and his eyes danced. Standing, he scooped her into his arms and effortlessly lifted her up the stairs and into the cabin. 'Sweetheart, I hate to break it to you, but, from this point on, there will only ever be one bed between us.'

Thea sighed, linked her arms around his neck and kissed his jaw. 'I can live with that,' she told him on a happy sigh. And as Farrell finally covered her mouth with his, she thought about how they'd started with one bed, and somehow ended up with everything.

* * * * *

If you enjoyed this story, check out this other great read from Joss Wood

For Business…or Pleasure

Available now!

Get up to 4 Free Books!

We'll send you 2 free books from each series you try
PLUS a free Mystery Gift.

Both the **Harlequin®** Historical and **Harlequin®** Romance series feature compelling novels filled with emotion and simmering romance.

YES! Please send me 2 FREE novels from the Harlequin Historical or Harlequin Romance series and my FREE Mystery Gift (gift is worth about $10 retail). I may cancel anytime by emailing ReaderServiceInfo@Harlequin.com or by calling 1-800-873-8635. If I don't cancel, I will receive 5 new Harlequin Historical books every month and be billed just $6.39 each in the U.S. or $7.19 each in Canada, or 4 new Harlequin Romance Larger-Print books every month and be billed just $7.19 each in the U.S. or $7.99 each in Canada, a savings of 20% off the cover price. It's quite a bargain! Shipping and handling is just 75¢ per book in the U.S. and $1.75 per book in Canada.* I understand that accepting the free books and gift places me under no obligation to buy anything—they are mine to keep for free no matter what I decide.

Choose one:
☐ Harlequin Historical (246/349 BPA G3CD)
☐ Harlequin Romance Larger-Print (119/319 BPA G3CD)
☐ Or Try Both! (246/349 & 119/319 BPA G3CE)

Name (please print)

Address   Apt. #

City   State/Province   Zip/Postal Code

Email: Please check this box ☐ if you would like to receive newsletters and promotional emails from Harlequin Enterprises ULC and its affiliates. You can unsubscribe anytime.

Mail to the Harlequin Reader Service:
IN U.S.A.: P.O. Box 1341, Buffalo, NY 14240-8531
IN CANADA: P.O. Box 603, Fort Erie, Ontario L2A 5X3

Want to explore our other series or interested in ebooks? Visit www.ReaderService.com or call 1-800-873-8635.

*Terms and prices subject to change without notice. Prices do not include sales taxes, which will be charged (if applicable) based on your state or country of residence. Canadian residents will be charged applicable taxes. Offer not valid in Quebec. This offer is limited to one order per household. Books received may not be as shown. Not valid for current subscribers to the Harlequin Historical or Harlequin Romance series. All orders subject to approval. Credit or debit balances in a customer's account(s) may be offset by any other outstanding balance owed by or to the customer. Please allow 4 to 6 weeks for delivery. Offer available while quantities last.

Your Privacy — Your information is being collected by Harlequin Enterprises ULC, operating as Harlequin Reader Service. For a complete summary of the information we collect, how we use this information and to whom it is disclosed, please visit our privacy notice located at https://corporate.harlequin.com/privacy-notice. Notice to California Residents—Under California law, you have specific rights to control and access your data. For more information on these rights and how to exercise them, visit https://corporate.harlequin.com/california-privacy. For additional information for residents of other U.S. states that provide their residents with certain rights with respect to personal data, visit https://corporate.harlequin.com/other-state-residents-privacy-rights.

HHHRLP2603